He, Levi Hunter, would *not* be riding a mule!

Not today, or any other day. The stubborn Ms. DeLisle could bank on that, he muttered to himself.

His boots crunched on gravel as he stepped off the porch. "What the hell?" he swore as he eyed a string of long-eared mules.

Franzi straightened from checking a loose girth buckle, returning his disdainful look across the animal's back. "I see the shower didn't help. One hour not enough sleep for you, Marshal, or are you always surly before breakfast?" She gathered the reins of her mount and swung easily into the saddle. "Let's move it," she ordered.

Levi continued to stare at the second saddled mule. "You don't actually intend for *me* to ride that?"

"You'd rather walk?"

Dear Reader,

I must admit I've always been enchanted by the vivid colors of desert sunsets and the elusive beauty of desolate cattle ranches. All right, so I'd be lying if I didn't include liking the subtle appeal of those lean-hipped cowboys. But I come by all of these interests honestly.

Before my mother married, she homesteaded a hundred and sixty acres in eastern Oregon—at a time when it was generally accepted that a woman's place on a ranch was at a hot wood stove, turning out three squares a day for huge threshing crews of hungry males. Is it any wonder I lean toward creating strong, feisty heroines like Franzi DeLisle? I like competent women who drive traditional males—in this instance, hero Levi Hunter—to distraction. Blame it on my genes.

So why a book about mules, you ask? Darned if I know. Except that I have friends in Kansas who talk mules a lot. They even dragged me out in a storm once to see a spindly legged Appaloosa mule—and he was a beauty. I was already trying to come up with a way of using him in a book, when fate landed me in a wonderfully Western California town that proclaimed itself "the Mule Capital of the World."

What if... I kept muttering over breakfast, my eye on the distant Sierra Nevadas, my thoughts on spotted-rumped mules. Suddenly, in sauntered one of those cowboys I mentioned earlier. Even as my husband accused me of drooling into my *huevos rancheros,* in waltzed the prettiest deputy sheriff either of us had ever seen. So much for breakfast, mine *and* hubby's. Now I ask you, is it in the genes—or the jeans?

Roz Denny

P.S. I'd be delighted to hear from readers! You can reach me at
3520 Knickerbocker #224, San Angelo, Texas 76904.

STUBBORN AS A MULE

Roz Denny

Harlequin Books

TORONTO • NEW YORK • LONDON
AMSTERDAM • PARIS • SYDNEY • HAMBURG
STOCKHOLM • ATHENS • TOKYO • MILAN
MADRID • WARSAW • BUDAPEST • AUCKLAND

ISBN 0-373-03276-5

Harlequin Romance first edition August 1993

STUBBORN AS A MULE

Printed in U.S.A.

CHAPTER ONE

"... AND SO IT IS that Gage DeLisle came from dust, and to dust he shall return..." Reverend Hanscomb's words drifted on the gentle breeze, his droning voice more hypnotic than soothing.

Lisa Callan's muffled sobs, along with the rattle of red earth striking Gage's coffin, pulled Franzi DeLisle's attention back to the grim reality of her brother's death.

Reaching out, Franzi steadied the distraught younger woman. Nineteen-year-old Lisa had dated Gage for six months—longer than most of his girlfriends lasted, so perhaps her display of emotion was genuine. But short alliances were typical of the happy-go-lucky Gage's attitude toward life. Still, Franzi had loved him unconditionally.

She found herself studying the somber crowd. Half of Jessup had turned out this first day of spring to pay respects to their young sheriff. For them, Gage's badge had outweighed his often irresponsible life-style. Franzi suspected she was the only one here today who believed the most irresponsible thing Gage had done in his short life was to become sheriff in the first place.

A scant three years his elder, she resented those who'd voted in favor of giving twenty-five-year-old Gage a badge. Heaven help her, but she resented him for taking it—and for dying.

Dust scattered as three deputies—kids, really—each dropped a handful of earth onto the coffin and filed past with badges shining. To Franzi the scene was like a replay of an old script.

First Uncle Mark. Then her father. Now Gage. Franzi pressed her palms together and stared at the uneven ground. Like his father and his uncle, both sheriffs before him, her brother had died young. And his death was equally wasteful. Wasteful and senseless. Senseless because Franzi knew that the sixteen-year-old punk who'd shot Gage in the attempted robbery of a convenience store would face perhaps six months' detention at best. Or he could be back on the streets tomorrow. Her own brief stint as a deputy of Alano County had taught her that.

Franzi tried to block out Lisa's wail. Then, blessedly, the ordeal of the ceremony ended. To her amazement she'd made it through another DeLisle funeral without losing control.

Immediately following the Reverend's closing, Alano County Commissioner Daryl Parker caught her sleeve. Franzi recognized the unconcealed pity in his eyes and steeled herself against another of his perfunctory condolences.

"Damn shame, Franzi. Damn shame."

Nodding agreement, she looked away and gave his outstretched hand a cursory touch. She smoothed a straying copper curl beneath her black mourning shawl, then tightened her grip on Lisa's bowed shoulders. "Could we save this talk for the ranch, Daryl? I expect there'll be a group heading out there now."

Placing a beefy hand on her arm, the commissioner detained her in spite of her plea. "This can't wait, Franzi." He thrust a curled hand in front of her face, flashing a worn silver star for both Franzi and Lisa to see. A deep crease almost rendered the words "Alano County, California" unreadable.

Franzi blanched and Lisa covered her face with both hands.

"You should have buried it with him, Daryl," Franzi said tightly.

"Ah...but I'm appointing you to fill Gage's shoes for the duration of his term, Franzi-girl." He pressed the cold metal into her hand. "It's your duty."

She drew back sharply. "Duty? You dare speak to *me* of duty?" She shoved the badge away and nudged Lisa toward the street. Squaring her shoulders, she stopped abruptly and turned back. "Jessup has extracted every last drop of DeLisle blood it's going to get. I don't even care to discuss Gage's benefits. Just mail me the information."

The commissioner followed at her heels as a host of mourners tipped their hats and hurried past. Franzi would have welcomed any interruption, but everyone seemed content to leave the recently bereaved women in the care of their esteemed commissioner.

Daryl Parker's next remark was as cold as his eyes. "There are no benefits for a man's bastard child, Franzi."

She stopped dead. "Child?" Her puzzled gaze flashed first to Daryl, then followed his to Lisa.

"Now, Franzi-girl. If you was to fill out Gage's term, I might be able to persuade our town council to overlook the small matter of a marriage license. Those old boys might even cough up some cash out of their own pockets so the little lady won't starve—for your daddy's sake. If you get my drift."

Franzi collapsed against her aging pickup. "Daryl. You can't force me to take that badge! Not even by spreading lies about Gage and Lisa."

His voice rose to chase her. "If you didn't bury yourself out on the ranch with those damned mules, Franzi, you'd have heard the whole town talking. Likely you'd know old man Callen's threatening to disown her, too."

Lisa's shoulders slumped. Her weeping grew hysterical. "My father won't listen," she blubbered, "and neither will Billy Lee. Gage married me, Franzi. I swear it. We drove to

Tijuana two weeks ago." She hiccuped and scrubbed her eyes. "Gage must have misplaced our license. But he was the one who said we'd get married—so people wouldn't talk. And he was gonna tell you soon, Franzi, honest." Lisa laced her fingers protectively across her abdomen.

Franzi sighed audibly, accepting the fact that there was no proof of her brother's marriage. She lifted her chin and glared at the man who'd delivered the news. "Placing blame at this late date will serve no purpose, Daryl. My brother's dead, and Lisa is scared and grieving."

Parker shrugged.

"Well, I know what it's like to be scared even if you don't," Franzi declared. "And I've certainly learned the hard way about grieving." She hugged Lisa, her heart aching for the girl—soon to be a mother—Gage had left behind. "You're likely right about one thing, though. If I'd been less *buried* at the ranch, I might have seen where things were headed. Even if I couldn't have made Gage listen, at the very least I might have warned Lisa how foolish it is to get involved with a lawman."

"Be that as it may, Franzi-girl," Parker insisted, "this town needs you."

"You've got three junior deputies. Forget me." She wrenched open the door of the pickup.

But Jessup's commissioner wasn't ready to give up. "You know those three are still green kids. Not a brain between them." His jaw hardened. "You were a deputy under Wade DeLisle—the best sheriff Jessup ever had. Oh, I know—" he put up a hand "—some folks said Wade might still be alive except for you, but I wasn't one of them. Now, you take your time and think on it real careful before you answer. Might be a chance to prove everyone wrong. Wipe the slate clean."

Damn the man. He hit below the belt. Feeling sick, Franzi helped the younger woman into the truck. She dug into her black shoulder bag and pulled out a ring of keys. As soon as she'd marshaled her senses and was able to speak, she lowered a window. "The best, as you call him, also trained Uncle Mark and Gage. Why is it, Commissioner, that the best die young?"

He couldn't seem to meet her eyes.

"That's what I thought—you don't have an answer," she said. "If Lisa wants, she can live with me. I may not have much to offer, but I expect it's better than your kind of generosity—with its price tag. At least, there's a good possibility I'll be around to help raise Gage's baby. Excuse us, please, we're needed at the ranch."

The big man deftly sailed Gage's badge through the window and onto her lap. "Talk it over with Lisa on the way home. She may cotton to the idea of people thinking she's a bona fide widow. I'm not asking you for a lifetime commitment, Franzi. Just a few months—until I can scout the other towns and get somebody on the next ballot who's qualified. Keep in touch, girl." He tipped his charcoal Stetson toward her, then resettled it and strode away without a backward glance.

Lisa huddled in a corner of the seat and looked miserable.

It didn't matter what the girl did or didn't cotton to, Franzi thought. One day could span a lifetime in a lawman's world, and she had lived with insecurity as long as she was going to. So what if her companions of choice happened to be the four-footed kind? For one thing, they could be counted on to meet her at the fence every day. She'd worked hard to gain their trust.

Tears, so long held at bay, finally threatened. She would welcome Lisa's company—since she didn't expect to marry. Oh, she'd once harbored romantic dreams, but she'd abandoned them after learning more about the men around Jessup. She hadn't met one who didn't ridicule her choice of profession. Especially when her new line of Appaloosa mules had begun to gain so much recognition at the shows.

But then, Gage had always maintained that this part of the country attracted "men's men"—as if that somehow made allowance for their faults. She, for one, didn't think it did. As far as she was concerned, the men around here were a century out of date in their attitudes toward women. *And* mules.

She'd given up trying to explain to the DeLisle men how she felt each time a mare foaled, how the new life gave her some sense of permanence. They might have scorned her animals, but mules were strong and sturdy, and they lived to a ripe old age. Apparently men, the men in *her* life, didn't give much thought to longevity.

Franzi sighed and stuffed Gage's badge into her coat pocket. "Lisa," she ventured, "do you feel like talking? It might help if I had all the facts."

The pickup's engine droned reassuringly. Lisa sat up and smoothed the front of her wrinkled cotton dress. "Gage treated me right, Franzi." Her voice sounded tiny. Hesitant. "I loved him. I didn't trap him. He said he liked the idea of adding a branch to the family tree." Biting her lip, the younger woman turned to face Franzi. "We *were* married. I know my dad's saying around town that Gage was trifling with me, but he's just afraid of losing a cook and housekeeper. That's all I've been to him since my mother died."

Franzi slowed the truck for an amber light. On impulse, she reached over and squeezed Lisa's hand. "It's all right. I'm not judging you. Gage wasn't bad, just careless. He would have come through eventually."

Huge tears rolled unchecked down Lisa's cheeks. "You *don't* believe me, either. Gage must have put that certificate somewhere to keep it safe. I saw him fold it to fit his wallet. Billy Lee said it wasn't there when they went through Gage's things. Oh, why did he die, Franzi? Why?"

Gripping the steering wheel until her knuckles were white, Franzi turned off the highway and onto her property.

Shadow Mountain Ranch—five hundred acres nestled at the foothills of the snowcapped Sierra Nevadas—had been in her family since her grandfather's day. Now it was hers.

"We're home, Lisa," she announced, a little too brightly. "I'll park over there near the barn, beside Henry's truck." She pointed to the dilapidated vehicle belonging to her one and only ranch hand.

The girl nodded. "I need a minute to pull myself together. I'm not as brave as you, Franzi."

For the briefest of moments, Franzi's heart screamed that she wasn't brave, either. And if Lisa was lucky, the seed planted in her womb would sprout a female. Wade DeLisle had joked often enough about how all DeLisle men were born wearing silver stars.

Franzi flung open the door with more force than necessary and helped Lisa down. Daryl Parker could go to hell and take his job with him. She was never, ever going to pin on that badge. Nothing was worth the risk.

THE COMMISSIONER'S daily calls were a testimony to his persistence. It didn't seem to matter that Franzi refused to talk to him, throwing herself, instead, into long days working her mules. Lisa kept to the house, and gradually the two women drifted into a sort of loose routine.

It was late in April, nearly four weeks after Gage's funeral, when Franzi was awakened from one of her better nights of sleep by the sound of her brother's dog growling deep in his throat. Pirate, so named by Gage because of a patch of black around one eye, had taken to dividing his nights between his master's old room, where Lisa now slept, and Franzi's ground-floor bedroom, where he seemed more at home with her familiar scent.

Blinking sleepily, Franzi did her best to make sense of the mosaic of moonlight flickering in patterns across the painted ceiling.

Twice the big Dalmatian stalked, still growling between the window and her bed before Franzi became conscious of other sounds—what might have been a stealthy footstep, followed by the scrape of a tree branch.

Leaning on one elbow, she picked up the illuminated clock. Two-thirty! Almost three hours before her day officially began. Perhaps Henry had been trying to wake her. She did have two mares almost ready to foal.

Throwing back the thin sheet, she slid out of bed and waited for his tap at her window. Pirate's sudden volley of barking would have drowned out a cannon. With a sharp command, she silenced the dog and pulled back the drapery, gazing uneasily outside. The shadowy outline of Mount Markham rose solidly in the distance, steady and reassuring. Tall ponderosa pines cast dark silhouettes across the clearing. That, too, was normal. Yet, for no reason at all, she shivered.

To the left, in the general direction of barns and paddock, a mule brayed and a horse whinnied. The ordinary predawn sounds calmed her. Beside her, Pirate growled again—a rumble from deep in his belly.

"It's okay, fella." Franzi quieted him with a pat on the head. "The first full moon makes everyone edgy." She let the curtain fall.

He licked her hand and left her side to pace impatiently in front of the bedroom door. "All right." Her yawn choked off a chuckle. "You win." She stretched the kinks out of her back, then caught up her thick, copper-colored hair, swiftly braiding it into a single plait down her back. "I'm sure it's nothing," she told the dog, "but if it'll make you happy, pal, we'll look in on Lisa, then do a quick tour outside. Come on, you ungrateful hound," she murmured, yawning again. "Lord, I'll be loading up on coffee all day just to stay awake."

Franzi quietly opened the door to Lisa's room and peered in. She watched Gage's woman-child sleep—hands over her head, palms curled like a baby. Backing out into the kitchen, she silently closed the door.

Lisa's father hadn't called or come by once. The girl spent her days searching for proof of a marriage she stubbornly insisted had taken place. But after they'd torn apart Gage's room and found nothing, Franzi had stopped looking. The best thing she could do now was help raise her brother's baby with more self-discipline.

"Okay, okay, Pirate, I'm coming," Franzi whispered.

Making her way through the dark dining room, she hesitated a moment beside Gage's gun cabinet. He'd often cautioned her to take a gun when she went to the barns alone at night, but she couldn't bring herself to do it. It wasn't easy to forget that bullets had snuffed out the lives of three robust DeLisles. "Anyway, you'll protect me, won't you, boy?" Franzi rubbed the dog's ears. "Oh, darn," she sighed. "I can't go out like this. Let me grab a pair of jeans from the dryer, then I'll be set."

Franzi tugged fresh jeans over a cotton-knit teddy, slid into moccasins and followed the anxious dog into the yard.

The wind had grown brisk, and the moon was now nearly hidden by a smattering of clouds. When Pirate silently faded into the darkness, Franzi cursed under her breath. "You'd better not get it into your head to go exploring or you'll find yourself learning how to use a doggie door."

In the distance, she heard an owl hoot. It was answered by a mate closer by. The mournful sound sent another chill up her spine. "Why didn't I grab a flashlight?" she muttered.

"Pirate," she called softly. "Come here. Where are you, boy?"

The forest stilled. At least from this new vantage point, she could see a dim light shining at the rear of Henry's cabin. Not normally given to fear without reason, she trotted toward the foaling barn, telling herself she was just being stupid. No doubt Henry was with one of the mares, already ushering in a new life.

Rounding the corner, she came to an abrupt stop. The foaling barn was pitch-black. Reflexively her damp fingers balled into fists.

Somewhere behind her, Pirate set up a frenzied barking. Young mules in the nearby weaning barn bugled in unison.

Stifling a jittery laugh, Franzi jogged briskly between the larger barns toward one of the sheds where a bare bulb glimmered. Why hadn't Henry turned on the outside floodlights? More than likely, he thought they needed to cut costs—especially now that they didn't have Gage's salary to help pay bills. What Henry didn't know was how fast Gage had gone through his money. She'd always made sure the ranch paid for itself. She'd mention it to the old man while it was fresh in her mind.

Franzi moistened her lips to call, not wanting to surprise him. But his name didn't get past the tip of her tongue. Pirate's snarls, coupled with a man's rough swearing, sent her flat up against the plank siding of the toolshed. Her heart almost leapt from her chest. She tried desperately to make her breath come quietly as she waited for a gut-wrenching curl of anxiety to pass. Sweat trickled between her breasts, and her stomach seemed to be turning cartwheels.

Franzi knew immediately that something was terribly wrong. Henry Ruiz was the gentlest of souls. She'd never heard him swear at anything.

As she gathered courage to take a closer look, there came a sickening thud. Pirate let out a pained yelp. Then all was silent.

Pirate! Franzi's stomach flipped.

Seconds later, she heard the furtive scrape of a saddle against the rack. Terrified, she clung to the rough siding. *There was a horse thief in her barn.*

Franzi closed her eyes and tried to think. Was this thief alone or did he have partners posted somewhere as lookouts? Bile rose in the back of her throat and the years fell away. All she could see were the cattle thieves who'd killed her father.

"No! Snap out of it, Franzi," she commanded under her breath. Using her forearm, she blotted her damp brow.

Without warning, the side door of the barn opened with a crash. Some part of her brain registered that her back was being gouged by the shed's rough planks and her nose itched unmercifully. Her knees shook and she sucked in an already concave stomach, trying to make herself invisible.

She heard a horse whicker. "Cricket." Franzi swallowed her favorite mare's name rather than speaking it. Cricket was a four-year-old honey of an Appaloosa, who had just produced her most promising mule colt yet.

The threat of losing years of careful breeding, to say nothing of a favorite pet, was almost enough to make her confront a would-be thief on the spot. Almost—but not quite.

Just then the moon broke through the clouds and Franzi saw a horse and rider, followed by a pack mule, pass the outer corral and melt into the darkness provided by a thick stand of lodgepole pine. Big and burly, the rider appeared to have some sort of kerchief knotted around his head. Although she'd caught only a fleeting glimpse before the shadows claimed her intruder, it was enough to make her skin crawl.

For a heart-stopping moment, she welcomed the security of the harsh planks. But as silence returned, worry for Henry and Pirate crowded out her fear. Were they both somewhere in the barn? Injured?

Franzi stepped from the safety of her shelter and saw something white flash in the darkness. She drew back. But it was only Henry, thank goodness. Still dressed in his nightshirt, feet bare of his usual boots, he came tearing across the clearing. The old bowlegged cowboy brandished an ancient rifle—a piece he claimed had been in his family since the Alamo. Under other circumstances, Franzi might have laughed at the comical picture he presented. Now, however, she was just relieved to see him alive.

Then she worried that his wild flight might trigger the asthma that plagued him. "Henry...stop!" she called, dashing out to meet him.

"That's one bad dude." The old cowboy struggled to speak. Pausing, he steadied himself with the rifle and gulped in air. "You okay, Missy D?" he choked, clutching his chest with a shaking hand.

Before Franzi could answer, the moon decided to show its full face. "Henry, you're hurt," she exclaimed, catching sight of a bloody goose egg nearly closing the old man's right eye. *"What happened?"*

He touched his eye experimentally and winced. "I heard a noise outside my cabin. I thought it was you come to wake me."

He gasped for air again and she placed an arm around his shoulders. "I jumped out of bed, hit the lights, then went to see. Bam, took a punch in the head from the ugliest dude I ever seen. Didn't know nothin' till I came round. Took me a few minutes to figure out he stole a pack, a gun, some food and even that carton of dynamite we just bought. I went and called Billy Lee. That danged-fool kid started askin' a passel of stupid questions. Said he hadda fill out a report. That's when I heard Pirate settin' up a fuss and I said for that rascally kid to get hisself out here, *muy pronto.*"

"So is Billy Lee coming?" Franzi interrupted her hand's laborious story.

"I guess." He sighed and slipped to one knee.

Nerves already frayed, Franzi jumped when she heard a rustling sound behind her. She turned and saw Pirate slithering out of the barn on his belly. By the flickering light of the moon, she could see his side was matted with blood.

Franzi didn't know which of them to help first, Henry or Pirate. But Henry seemed to be breathing better and Pirate put his head on his paws and gazed up at her with sad eyes. "Do you feel good enough to help me get Pirate to the house, Henry? I'll need to check him out and maybe call the vet. We'll call a doctor to look at you, too." She stopped as another thought loomed. "Henry...what if that man comes back? Do you have any idea who he was?"

Henry had crouched down beside the dog when light beams from an approaching automobile streaked across the clearing and bounced off the barn, temporarily blinding both of them.

The vehicle was shrouded in dust and going full throttle as it took the corner on two wheels and skidded onto De-Lisle land.

Franzi held her breath. The driver obviously had little control and less sense.

"Must be Billy Lee," shouted Henry, suddenly finding enough wind to jump up and wave his arms high over his head.

Pirate whined and Franzi dropped down to stroke his ears.

"It's not Billy Lee's truck," she said anxiously. What if their night caller had hooked up with a friend over the ridge? What if two of them had decided to come back for the rest of her stock—and finish off any witnesses? A knot of fear coiled in her stomach. Who would take care of Lisa and the baby if something happened to her?

She threw up both hands to shield her eyes from the glaring headlamps. A muddy black Bronco squealed to a stop no more than three feet from where she knelt, hunched over her pet, protecting him from bits of flying gravel thrown by the huge, off-road tires.

For no reason that she could understand, Franzi's apprehension dissolved and sprang to new life as annoyance. When the driver's door flew open, she bristled. Dangerous or not, this predawn visitor would not find her an easy mark. "Get behind me, Henry," she ordered. "I'll do the talking."

Warily, a tall, rangy man—a stranger—disembarked, his hands outstretched and empty.

Henry's leathery fingers inched toward his discarded gun.

Franzi tried, too late, to stop him. Anyone with half a brain could see the corroded antique was no threat. But a stranger might act without thinking.

Henry's shaking hand had barely reached the worn stock when the newcomer grabbed the old man's nightshirt and lifted him off his feet. In less than a wink, Henry was divested of his rifle, and Franzi was left blinking up at a set of wide shoulders blocking her view of the moonlight.

"Don't even think it, either of you." The stranger's gravelly voice gave fair warning. "Easy does it," he cautioned more softly, staying Franzi with a hand as she struggled to her feet. "Just sit tight till someone tells me what's going on." He took a small leather folder from his shirt pocket and flipped it open.

Antipathy stiffened Franzi's spine. She didn't need the shaft of light winking off the silver shield to know their visitor was a lawman. Every arrogant, take-charge line of the man's face and build screamed his profession.

"You're trespassing on private land," Franzi stated calmly as she turned to lift her pet. What she hadn't counted on was her knees shaking so hard she couldn't budge the animal's dead weight.

"My business here is official, ma'am," the man said politely. "I was in town talking to the local authorities when your call came through." He let go of Henry's nightshirt and returned his badge to his pocket. "I'll try to be quick with my questions."

Franzi's resentful gaze strayed to the dusty fabric of his black shirt. Matching black pants, having seen more than their fair share of washing, outlined lean hips. Her lip curled. She was generally one to judge a man by the look in his eyes—the way her father had taught her. But this lawman wore his Stetson pulled low on his forehead and it threw his eyes into unreadable shadow. She didn't like that. With a toss of her long braid, she ignored him and turned back to her pet.

"I said, hold on," he growled, shifting toward her.

Franzi heard the whisper of metal against leather and froze. Who did this joker think he was, drawing a weapon? She scrambled to her feet. Belatedly, and to her chagrin, she realized their visitor had only removed his jacket, then tossed it and Henry's old blunderbuss to the ground. Without invitation he knelt and easy-as-you-please gathered up the dog.

Franzi's breath stalled. From this range, she caught a flash of steel in his storm-gray eyes, seconds before the halo of the moon softened them to pewter.

"Explanations can wait," he muttered near her ear, "until the man and the dog get attended. Where to?"

Passing a tongue over dry lips, Franzi said nothing. Distracted as she was, she simply reached out to help Henry.

The old man whispered loud enough for the stranger to hear, "Shouldn't we ask who he is, Missy D?"

After a tense moment, in which the stranger's eyes clashed with her own, he reluctantly said, "The name's Levi Hunter. U.S. Marshal. Been almost a week trackin' a no-good by the name of Paul Eilert, known as Popeye. Lost him outside Jessup. A deputy in town directed me here when we got your call."

"Sorry," Franzi said curtly. "We can't help you." She moved to take Pirate, who by now seemed perfectly content in the man's strong arms.

"Not so fast." The marshal sidestepped her. "I'll carry him. He's way too heavy for you. There'll be time later for us to talk."

Something about the low rumble of the man's voice gave Franzi the impression of callused fingers brushing silk. A chill slithered up her spine, and some undefined emotion knotted her stomach. But she had only to remind herself of his profession and the tightness unwound with the precision of a well-thrown lariat. Not only was he a lawman, which was bad enough, he was a lawman on a mission, which was even worse.

"Let's go, Henry," she said, not caring if she sounded rude. He waved her on ahead. Once she determined Henry could indeed make it under his own power, she spun on the heels of her moccasins and walked briskly toward the house.

What she felt like doing was weeping, an uncharacteristic action for her. It might be due to losing Cricket. Perhaps it was the result of having dredged up old memories of her father. Or her recent grief and lack of sleep. Whatever the cause, Franzi resented the fact that the first man in a long while to make her stomach flutter belonged to the one occupation she abhorred.

Although concern for Henry and her dog dictated that she couldn't run away from him, the next best thing was to put as much distance between them as humanly possible. After a quick check to make certain Henry still followed, she picked up her pace.

The sooner she saw U.S. Marshal Levi Hunter on his way, the better off she'd be. Because Franzi knew that any tears she felt like shedding would be better spent on whatever brokenhearted women this stranger had left behind.

And one of these times, he'd leave forever. Of that Franzi had no doubt. For who knew better than she that *all* lawmen, by virtue of their profession, were careless of their women?

CHAPTER TWO

IN THE DAPPLED MOONLIGHT, Marshal Hunter watched the rhythmic sway of the woman's hips and tried desperately to remember what the fresh-faced deputy in town had said about the lady of Shadow Mountain Ranch.

Certainly not that she had hair as brilliant as a western sunset, or skin the color of newly drawn cream. And her eyes... His mind went completely blank for a moment. He was hard-pressed to find a suitable description for eyes that reminded him of the translucent crest of an ocean wave.

Levi tightened his hold on the dog, resulting in a muffled whine. "Easy boy," he soothed as he tried to recall if there'd been any discussion about the man of the house. Not that it mattered. The woman up ahead was about as tough and prickly as a cactus, while he was partial to ruffled skirts and lacy things. To gentle, feminine women. Like Amanda...

Unless she had a softer side she kept hidden. Levi surveyed the hip-hugging jeans with analytical detachment. Couldn't hide much there.

The woman neared the house, and the dog whimpered again. Levi stopped suddenly as the hips he'd been following disappeared with a swish through an unlocked door. Her utter lack of caution lit a flare of anger in his stomach. However, before he could formulate a lecture on safety, her anxious face reappeared and she beckoned him inside.

Levi edged past her into a dimly lit kitchen. As she stood at the door and waited for the old man, Levi took the time to peer cautiously into the room's shadowy corners.

Amanda Farrell had never locked doors, either. Remembering his first love brought Levi a swift pang of sorrow. But it made the lecture he needed to deliver infinitely easier. "Bad habit, ma'am, leaving your house unlocked."

"The name is DeLisle, not ma'am," Franzi snapped, letting the screen door slam. "We don't often get strangers this far out of town. The ones who do stumble in are generally lost and appreciate our hospitality." Impatiently she looked out again. "Henry," she called. "Do you need help?"

Levi wasn't so tired he didn't understand she was telling him to mind his own business.

Henry limped past her, still huffing from the fast pace set by the others. Oblivious to Franzi's glaring match with the marshal, he stepped between them. "Pirate don't look so good, Missy D. I'll call Doc Varner pronto." Not waiting for her response, he snatched up the wall phone and punched out a number.

"Henry, let me do that," Franzi protested. "You sit. I'll check Pirate. But what about you? Shouldn't you see Doc Baines?"

He shook his head.

Frowning, she turned to flick on the overhead light and seek out a place where Hunter could put the dog. She bumped into him and her words died away. Outside, under the stars, she hadn't noticed the dark sooty rings circling his light gray irises. Now, in the harsher light of the kitchen, she found the combination compelling. Or maybe unnerving was more apt. So unnerving, in fact, that she immediately turned all her attention to her pet. "Since Henry insists on calling," she said stiffly, caressing the dog's head, "I'll go fetch an old quilt from the laundry room and you can put him on the floor. He must be getting heavy."

Levi smiled. "Not bad." He purposely left off calling her ma'am. "While we're waiting," he added, "do you think you could fill me in on what happened out there? The mutt's pretty bloody and your man's got a knot on his head the size of Gibraltar."

Franzi cut him off. "Pirate is not a mutt. And don't you think it's a little crass talking business before we get these two some help?"

"Crass?" His eyes widened. "This from the woman who keeps her doors unlocked for every Tom, Dick and Harry? Excuse me. I thought I was expressing concern."

Her jaw tightened. "I rather imagine your concern is for your *mission,* Marshal." Franzi disappeared through an alcove to search for an old quilt. By the time she returned, Henry was off the phone. "Can Varner come?" she asked, making a production out of fluffing the blanket out on the floor. "I know you don't like doctors, Henry," she said, "but call Baines, anyhow."

The old wrangler's reply was lost in a squeal of brakes outside. Seconds later there was a loud hammering on the back door.

Henry limped over and yanked it open. "Howdy, Billy Lee," he greeted. "What's up? You look like someone with his tail caught in a stampede."

"Howdy yourself, Henry. Whaddaya mean, what's up? I rushed out here 'cause it sounded urgent." The young deputy stepped inside, pausing to remove his hat. Fine blond hair fell over one eye. In a nervous gesture, he tossed his head and flipped the errant strands aside, only to have them droop again.

"Hey, Marshal." He flashed a grin at Levi. "I see you found your way to Shadow Mountain." Billy Lee closed the door behind him. "Any leads on your suspect?" As he crossed the room, his gaze skipped over Franzi, on her knees examining the dog, then skidded back to linger. Showing marked concern, the young deputy took in the dirty rifle on the counter and Henry's battered face. "What the hell happened here?"

"Precisely my question, Deputy," Levi drawled.

Billy looked at Franzi. "I'd have come sooner, except I had to go pick up old man Farnsworth from the tavern. The bartender confiscated his damn car keys so he wouldn't end up a menace on the highway. As usual, his wife raised Cain and demanded we drive him home. You know how Verna is," he apologized to Franzi. Peering around, he asked abruptly, "Where's Lisa?"

"Asleep, I hope," Franzi said dryly, touching a finger to her lips.

"Maybe you can get their story, Deputy." Levi sounded more than a little exasperated as he knelt opposite Franzi. "I just want to know if they've seen Eilert." By now, though, he wasn't certain that statement was entirely true. He'd been wondering who Lisa was since Billy mentioned the name—was she this woman's child? If so, where was her husband while she was roaming dark corrals?

"Well, have you?" Billy asked, not realizing that Franzi had jumped up and was on the telephone to the family doctor.

Levi rocked back on his haunches and hung both wrists over his knees as he watched her shrug. With a lazy stretch of one hand, he drew a thumb and forefinger over his tired eyes. Seeing the young deputy with his hat in hand, Levi realized he hadn't removed his own. He sighed and swept it from his head.

Franzi heard the sigh and shot him a quick glance. The way he stroked his face told her he'd passed normal endurance. How many times had she watched her father and Gage do the same? Too many. And although she wouldn't dream of asking, she wondered how long this big tough marshal thought he could run on nothing but guts.

Ignoring Billy's repeated question, Franzi hung up and avoided thinking that her intruder and the marshal's quarry might be the same man. Surely a fed from the big city would have bigger fish to land than some petty horse thief. Then she remembered the cruel set of the intruder's lips, and a small doubt crossed her mind. She brushed it aside. Whatever the marshal's business, it didn't concern her, and she just wished he'd get on with it.

"Henry," she said suddenly, "I think you should lie down with an ice pack until the doctor comes. You look pale."

The old wrangler shook his shaggy gray head. "I'm fine, boss. Quit fussin'."

"At least sit down at the table while I brew a pot of coffee," she pleaded. "Billy Lee, maybe he'll sit if you do. And, Marshal," she said, taking charge, "you should have a seat before you keel over." She yanked out a straight-backed chair. "When the coffee's done, I'll bring it."

"Forget the coffee. I just need answers," Hunter said. However, he did take the chair.

Lisa chose that moment to stumble out of her bedroom. Without looking right or left, she stifled a wide yawn with her hand. She opened her eyes and saw Franzi making coffee. "Did I oversleep?" she asked in surprise. "I didn't hear the alarm. I wasn't shirking, Franzi, honest."

"Lisa," Franzi said sharply, "It's all right. I was up, anyway. But where's your robe?" Although there was nothing terribly revealing about the young woman's cotton pajamas, Franzi thought it might embarrass her once she discovered their guests.

"I never wear one. You know that, Franzi." Lisa looked puzzled.

Franzi's gaze slid behind Lisa to the marshal, who suddenly straightened in his seat. "Uh . . . Lisa, we have company," she stammered.

It figures, she thought nastily. Like Gage, Hunter had an eye for the ladies. Nonplussed, Lisa spun, then treated the stranger to a bright smile. "Oh, hello there. I didn't see you. Sorry." She did a double take. "Henry? And Billy Lee, too?" Coyly she asked, "What brings you here? Three times in one week, Billy. It's becoming a habit."

So this was Lisa, Hunter thought. In truth, he barely gave the pregnant girl a glance. Instead, he was testing the cadence of Franzi's name as it fell from Lisa's lips.

"Ugh, what happened to him?" Lisa stopped beside the bloodied dog and threw a hand over her mouth. She sidled closer to Billy Lee's chair. He stood immediately and steadied her with an arm around her waist.

"Pirate surprised an intruder, Lisa." Franzi slapped the lid on the coffee can. "About that robe . . ." she said pointedly. "Borrow mine." She knew she sounded curt, but that was because it was news to her just how many times Billy Lee had been out to the ranch lately. No wonder Daryl wanted her to take the job, if he couldn't keep better tabs on his deputies than that.

Gathering mugs, she carried them to the table. How Lisa could even consider taking up with another lawman was beyond her. "The robe is in my closet," she reminded the girl.

Hunter looked up at her and arched a brow.

Franzi glared back and smacked the mugs down so hard in front of him a chip flew from the bottom of one. "Since you're in such an all-fired hurry, Marshal, why aren't you asking Henry those questions? Billy Lee, sit back down and listen," she ordered. "You may need this for your report."

Billy dropped his arm from Lisa and sat immediately.

Lisa threw a pout his way before flouncing off toward her room.

Having settled one issue, Franzi leaned back against the counter and crossed her arms. "Now, where were we, Marshal? I expect Billy Lee has better things to do than wait around here for daybreak—like, go home to his own bed."

"*We*," he stressed, "were nowhere. You're very good at giving orders," he said sarcastically, sweeping a lazy gaze the length of her. "I'm surprised you haven't given *me* any." His tired eyes lit for a moment on the loose thongs lacing her knit teddy. It took every bit of his self-discipline to look away.

Franzi felt her face flame and the heat extend to the keyhole opening of her skimpy top. He probably thought she had a lot of nerve telling Lisa to get a robe. One look at the uncompromising set of his mouth, and she lifted her chin and thrust out her jaw. She did give the orders around here, and she didn't owe this autocratic lawman any explanations.

The percolator emitted its last burp. Franzi snatched it up and splashed coffee into the four mugs. "I don't appreciate your humor, Hunter. Just get to the point."

"Be glad to, ma'am," he growled, "if you're through playing drill sergeant."

Henry and Billy chuckled. She shot them a dark glance that brought silence, then stomped over to the gun cabinet. She yanked open a drawer and took out a stale pack of cigarettes and lighter Gage had stashed there once when he was trying to give up smoking.

Having kicked the habit herself years ago, Franzi was irritated to find she'd let this lawman drive her to taking it up again. Still, it would give her something to do with her hands. Drawing one from the pack, she placed it between her lips and lit it with shaking fingers. "If you expect me to roll out a red carpet just because you flash that shiny silver badge, Hunter, you're in for a shock." She gestured impatiently, blowing smoke toward the ceiling. "Ask your questions, then get out." She made a show of puffing rapidly.

The smoke stung his eyes. "Give me one straight answer, Ms. DeLisle," he said, his control slipping, "and I'll be happy to go where I can breathe easier."

"I doubt our intruder and your man are one and the same." *There,* Franzi thought. *Was that straight enough for him?* All of a sudden she wasn't feeling so straight herself. Dizzy was more like it. It really had been a long time since she'd smoked.

Forcing a sickly smile to her lips, Franzi clasped an arm protectively beneath her breasts and said in a strained voice, "Henry seems to have a bit more color." Too bad she couldn't say the same for herself. "I'm sure he'll be happy to describe our th-thief." She choked then and her voice cracked.

Hunter's gaze narrowed. Was she all right?

Franzi mistook his concern for disapproval. So, the lawman didn't like women who smoked. Well, all the more reason to take it up again. She deliberately set up a smoke screen between them—and felt woozier by the minute.

"I think I'll go change into work clothes. Henry," she entreated faintly. "Will you ask Lisa to come for me when the doctors arrive?" Without waiting for his answer, Franzi dashed from the room. No matter how wretched she felt, she'd have died rather than let Hunter see her snuff the darn thing out.

Levi's gaze followed her from the room. *Whoa, Hunter. Hold everything!* He smoothed a hand over his three-day beard, then took a swig of the bitter black coffee, realizing why he'd never acquired a taste for the stuff. But he was just passing through, he reminded himself, not settling in. His first order of business was to bring in Mandy's assailant. "Okay, Henry," he directed, turning his attention to the old man, "tell me about your intruder."

"Biggest, ugliest dude I ever seen," said Henry, capturing both Hunter's and Billy's interest with that one observation. When Henry got to the part about the intruder stealing a loaded gun and the dynamite, Levi stood, picked up the coffeepot and poured a second round for the others, passing over his own cup, which was still half-full. Natural adrenaline was normally all he needed to get him through a chase, and this time he had even more than usual driving him. It set his teeth on edge just to think about Franzi DeLisle facing scum like Popeye. The knot that had formed in his stomach when he started this mission pulled tighter.

As it happened, the veterinarian and the rural doctor arrived and delayed the end of Henry's story. But Levi had heard enough to know Eilert had passed this way. If he didn't get a move on, the trail would be cold.

Fully dressed now, Lisa wandered back into the room. Henry promptly sent her in search of Franzi. When the two women walked in together, the vet was examining Pirate, the doctor had a stethoscope to Henry's chest, and Levi was in the process of asking Billy Lee for directions to Los Angeles.

Franzi paused behind him as she finished buttoning the cuffs of her flannel shirt. "Your man isn't heading toward L.A., Marshal," she said. She'd seen where he entered the trees. "He's traveling northwest—toward Sacramento, or maybe San Francisco." Continuing past the men, she dropped down beside her dog. "How is he, Doc?"

Levi slapped his dusty Stetson against his thigh. Presumably the scornful snort he issued was aimed at Franzi's comment.

"You'd better listen to her, Hunter," Billy Lee cautioned. "Franzi's about the best tracker in the state."

Levi ignored Billy, watching as Doc Varner wiped his hands on a towel. "Pirate's a tough critter," the vet said. "Looks to me like he took a nasty blow from a boot, but nothing's broken. I'll leave some antibiotics all the same. I expect he'll heal nicely."

Relief softened the tight lines around Franzi's mouth.

As she spoke to Doc Baines and Henry, Levi ran agitated fingers through his hair. Though small when compared to Eilert's other offenses, the injuries he'd inflicted here were typical of his cruelty.

Replacing his sweat-stained hat, Levi pulled the brim low and turned tired steps toward the door. "Deputy Lee, I'll take a look at that map you mentioned, the one showing back roads to the coast."

"Sure, Marshal."

Levi turned. "Before I forget, you did notify gas stations in the area to be on the lookout for the stolen vehicle we discussed, didn't you?"

Billy stepped out of the corner where he'd gone to join Lisa. Snapping his fingers, he unbuttoned his breast pocket and withdrew a wadded paper. "Meant to tell you first thing, Hunter, but I plumb forgot, what with all this." He waved a palm. "The state patrol picked up the car you reported stolen. It'd been abandoned on the highway north of Twin Lakes, maybe about one in the morning. Engine was smokin' to beat hell. Looks like she ran dry and blew a head gasket. Your man'll have to steal another set of wheels. When he does, we'll get him."

Levi stalked to the sink, swept aside the dotted swiss curtains over the window and squinted out at the still-dark sky. He sighed wearily. "Now I'll have to start from scratch again." He shook his head. These folks didn't seem to understand what type of man Eilert was, but he couldn't very well leave without telling them. "Paul Eilert," he began in a dispassionate voice, "is awaiting extradition to at least five states—all in connection with assaults and murder." He paused. "This was his fourth escape in two years."

What Levi held back was that if he hadn't been so anxious to see his brother-in-law's new stallion last week—if he hadn't trusted his partner to get Eilert to the airport alone—the felon would already be behind bars. And Mandy probably wouldn't be hovering between life and death.

Franzi was well acquainted with guilt of the variety she heard in Hunter's tone. She just didn't understand *why* he felt that way. "Didn't Henry tell you that your suspect helped himself to one of my horses and a pack filled with supplies?" Her voice was filled with the compassion he'd stirred in her.

Levi jerked back and the curtain fell. Fighting a desperate need for sleep, he resented both her nearness and what he heard as a soft-spoken rebuke. He also resented the faint curl of her perfume, which was luring him down an almost forgotten path.

"I don't recall that he mentioned much besides guns," Levi said curtly. "And dynamite. But the fact that he's on horseback only strengthens what I said before. He'll keep to the back roads between here and L.A."

Franzi felt his censure and didn't mind setting the marshal back on his heels. "Like I said, Hunter, your suspect isn't going to L.A. He's heading into high country. Come daybreak, we'll get a better fix on his route."

She was amazed at herself. What on earth had made her extend the olive branch? Was it the shadow of pain she'd glimpsed in his eyes, the self-condemnation she'd heard in his voice? But when he brushed past her with that damned professional detachment in place, she wanted to snatch back her rash offer.

Lisa tugged at Billy's sleeve. "Will someone please tell me what's going on? You aren't chasing some dangerous criminal, are you, Billy?"

He squeezed her shoulder reassuringly. "Don't worry yourself, angel. Everything's under control. In a couple of hours it'll be light. Franzi will go read some tracks. That's all."

Franzi's stomach tightened. Why hadn't she simply minded her own business? Why should she do anything to help Marshal Hunter get himself killed? The last thing she needed was another dead lawman on her conscience. Shaking her head, she crossed the room to check with Doc Baines on Henry's condition.

The old veterinarian, meanwhile, gathered his bags and ambled over to Franzi. "If you're planning one of your lengthy treks, Franzi-girl," he said, "you'd better leave Pirate at home. It'll be a while before he's up to a climb."

"I'm not going anywhere, Doc." She escorted both men to the door, fully believing her statement. "You'll send me your bills, gentlemen?"

They both grinned, nodded and left.

Levi listened with half an ear. He was studying the well-stocked arsenal in the locked gun cabinet. "I wish you didn't have these," he said abruptly. "All too often criminals turn a victim's own gun on him—or her." He frowned. "Innocent bystanders like you can get hurt." It'd been Adam's gun Eilert had used on Amanda.

"Franzi knows her way around guns," Billy Lee put in. "She won't slow you down."

"This isn't a job for a woman." Levi raised his voice. "Since we have no reason for further delay, Deputy, I say we get started. Now that Eilert's armed again, we can't afford to let him get too far."

"No!" Lisa stood on tiptoe and pulled Billy's face around until they were eye to eye. "Billy, you *promised*..." She didn't finish, but Billy obviously knew what he'd promised. He shifted uncomfortably from one foot to the other.

Franzi's sympathy was with Lisa.

Billy raked a hand through his hair. "I get lost in the foothills, Marshal, and I wouldn't last a day in the Sierras. Besides, I've been on duty all night. You ask Franzi to lead you. Beg her if you have to."

Levi took off his hat and smoothed the inside band. Cold tracking wasn't what he did best. But even if she was as capable as Billy claimed, he wouldn't place her in such danger. "I haven't slept a wink in two nights, Deputy, and it's not stopping me. Another thing—I don't beg women for anything. She's not going. Got that?"

Billy couldn't meet Hunter's steely gaze. Turning, he made a last silent appeal to Franzi.

Her eyes smoldered. "Don't look at me like *I'm* responsible, Billy Lee. Anyway, it's not as if Lisa's in any condition to give Henry a hand with the chores if I run off. Let him go on his suicide mission alone."

Franzi's old ranch hand, having been proclaimed sound by the doctor only moments before, pounded his barrel chest. "I'll do fine by myself, Missy D. You help find that bad dude." He grinned broadly, showing a tobacco-stained tooth.

"Franzi, it's not your job, either," Lisa rushed to say. "I mean, you turned Daryl down flat. Why would you change your mind?" Her voice shook.

Levi dropped his hat on a chair. "There's nothing to argue about here. No woman is chasing Paul Eilert." He faced Billy Lee, his hands dropping to bracket lean hips above a low-riding leather belt. "I hope your sheriff doesn't let you hide behind a woman's skirts."

With the light of battle in her eyes, Franzi matched his stance. "In case you haven't noticed, Marshal, I'm not wearing skirts."

His gaze drifted over her. "Oh, I've noticed. Well, pants don't make a man, Ms. DeLisle."

"How dare you! I've been leading tours into the high Sierras since I was old enough to throw a leg over a saddle. Sex has nothing to do with it, Marshal." She lifted her chin defiantly as Levi's eyebrows shot up.

Personally, he thought Franzi DeLisle had a way of looking as though sex had something to do with just about everything. But that was only part of the problem. The other was that her stubbornness instantly raised his masculine hackles, bringing protective instincts to the fore.

"Where I come from, we respect women too much to put them in danger."

"Really? Which planet is that, Marshal?" Franzi tapped her foot.

"Very funny, Ms. DeLisle," he shot back. "Salt Lake City, though I grew up farther south. As the only son in a family of six daughters, I learned to value women." His lips quirked ever so slightly.

"Oh." Franzi fell silent.

"Much as I'd like to pander to your ego, Ms. DeLisle, my job is to catch a murderer."

"My ego? You supercilious son of a—" Franzi broke off when she could see by his eyes that his anger wasn't really aimed at her. She licked her lips. "You have a personal reason for wanting this Eilert, don't you?"

He was standing close enough to Franzi to feel her warmth, a warmth that made the other people in the room fade from view. Suddenly, though, it wasn't green-eyed Franzi he was seeing, but a dark-eyed waif named Amanda Farrell. Although she'd chosen to marry his best friend, Adam Farrell, instead of him, she'd always held a special place in his heart. Feminine, funny, artistic Amanda. Since kindergarten, he and Adam had fought for, loved and protected her.

Yes, with Mandy in a coma, he guessed one could say his reason was personal all right. Levi reached out a callused finger toward Franzi's sun-kissed cheek, then let his hand drop before he touched her. He wanted to explain, but he didn't know where to begin. "There's a woman," he said softly. "Amanda . . ." His voice cracked. "She was . . ."

Franzi almost missed the woman's name, though she strained to hear. She stood without moving, all but forcing herself not to breathe—as if by not breathing she could will this conversation away. He cared a great deal for the woman, she could feel it.

"Was?" she probed after a moment, unable to help herself.

Levi's jaw worked.

Franzi wished with all her heart she could take her question back. There were depths to this man that frightened her, his pain was palpable.

"Popeye's criminal record spans twenty years," Levi said in a steadier voice. "He's one of those amoral characters who went straight from the playpen into the state pen. I doubt there's a crime on the books he hasn't committed."

"I still don't understand," Franzi murmured. "What about Amanda?"

"Shot." The single word exploded into the room.

"Pardon me?" Franzi's stomach curdled. "You mean she's dead?"

Across the room, Billy Lee and Lisa had stopped talking. Henry dropped heavily into a kitchen chair.

Levi paced the length of the room. "She was home by herself. Quilting. Eilert got a lousy thirty bucks in household money and a beat-up Ford pickup that fell apart no more than a hundred miles down the road. Mandy's condition is critical. She... may not make it."

Where yesterday, Franzi had been positive there wasn't enough empathy in her to make her ever touch a badge again, she now found herself wavering. His pain went deep—perhaps as deep as her own. Clearing her throat, she said, "You'd be a fool to head into the mountains before daylight, Hunter. I doubt your suspect has gotten very far himself." She glanced at the kitchen clock. "You could get, oh, maybe an hour's sleep. You'll be needing a mount, a full pack and a guide who knows the trails."

Coming alert, Levi tugged his sleeve back and checked his watch. "One hour. Are you saying you can get me a pack put together in that length of time? I'll pay you, of course."

Franzi chewed her lip. The pain-driven man of a moment ago was gone. In his place was the arrogant lawman. He'd quite pointedly ignored her offer to act as his guide. The smile she turned on him didn't quite reach her eyes. "Henry can throw something together. Lisa," she instructed quietly, "Please show the marshal to my room. But let him set the alarm himself. I wouldn't want us to be accused if by chance he oversleeps."

"Ah... a taste of the red-carpet treatment you mentioned when I first came in." His quick laugh rustled like dry leaves. "I'm not one of your lost souls," he said. "I know exactly where I'm going and why I'm here."

Franzi hardly needed to be reminded of his mission. If she had any sense, she'd toss him out on his ear. Instead, she fell back on sarcasm, muttering, "Enjoy your hour's sleep, Marshal—even if you're the big lawman who doesn't need any." She hadn't realized he'd stepped up behind her. Not until she heard his handcuffs drop into his hat.

"I've noticed you like having the last word," he said mildly. "Don't get any ideas, Ms. DeLisle. In one hour, I'll be leaving here. Alone."

Franzi wanted to smack him, but instead, she smiled. "You've only got fifty-five minutes left for sleeping, Hunter. I'd get at it, if I were you."

He spun on his heel and stalked off after Lisa, wondering why Franzi DeLisle felt she had to act so tough. It occurred to him that he'd get a glimpse of the real woman in the way she'd furnished her private quarters. Maybe he'd see some hint of a softer Franzi there.

Thanking Lisa, Levi stepped past her into the bedroom. He was unable to mask his disappointment. The room was spartan. Tired as he was, he took a moment to study the plain iron bedstead, the nondescript dresser and nightstand, both swept clean. Finally he sank onto the worn chenille spread and tugged off first one boot, then the other.

So he'd been wrong in thinking there was a softer side to her, he thought as he stripped off his shirt and pants. It was just that he'd been so sure she'd have some personal items, a few feminine trappings—diaries and photographs, jewelry and perfume—like his sisters had. But the room yielded nothing.

He closed his eyes and yawned. She'd still managed to have the last word out there. Shaking his head, Levi set the alarm, then turned off the light and steeled himself to meet rough muslin sheets, considering the frugality of everything else in the room.

His skin hit cool slick satin and he shot bolt upright.

Flopping over on his stomach, he buried his face in a soft pillow smelling faintly of honeysuckle and laughed out loud.

"Tomorrow," he muttered around a sleepy yawn, "tomorrow, we'll just see who gets the last word."

CHAPTER THREE

AN ALARM WITH A BUZZ that sounded like an angry bee pulled Levi Hunter from the depths of oblivion.

Yanking a pillow over his head, he reached out one arm and silenced it the same way he would have dealt with a bee—with a swift, merciless swat.

Savoring the silence, he groaned, trying to convince himself it was all a dream. It *must* be a dream; he'd only just closed his eyes, hadn't he? Levi drifted for a moment, fighting wakefulness. But where the alarm had failed, the faint scrape of a door brought him skyrocketing out from under sheet and pillow. He cast about for his pants, which were normally never more than arm's length away. This time his hand encountered only air.

"Rise and shine, Marshal. It's three minutes past daybreak and time's wasting."

Levi wasn't so tired he couldn't put a name to the lilting voice. Franzi DeLisle. He'd scarcely conjured up her image in his mind when the lady herself tore open the curtains and daylight flooded the room.

He threw up one arm to ward off the sudden stab of brilliance and felt the sheet slide.

"You'll have to eat breakfast on the trail, Marshal. Eilert will be moving fast, now that he can se—" turning from the window to face the bed, Franzi swallowed hard, barely stammering out the remainder of her sentence "—s-s-see where he's going." She stood gaping at Levi Hunter's well-muscled, beautifully bronzed and completely naked torso. "Ohh." Her fingers flew to cover her lips and she edged discreetly toward the door.

Levi lowered his arm, squinting against the light, and got a clear look at her crimson cheeks. He scrambled for the fallen sheet. "Ten minutes," he snapped. "I can be ready in ten minutes, Ms. DeLisle."

"Not a morning person, are we, Hunter?" Franzi recovered her aplomb. After all, she'd grown up in a house full of men. "Lisa washed and dried your things. You were dead to the world when she picked them up. Catch!" She threw him the worn denim pants and dark shirt. "Most of what you need should be in the bathroom. Gage left some things..." She knew she was talking too fast. He seemed to have this effect on her, and Franzi hated it. Grasping the knob, she hauled open the door. She'd seen Gage shirtless plenty of times. He'd had muscles and a tan, too. No big deal.

"What is it you think I need?" Levi asked around a yawn, somewhat confused by her sarcasm.

Franzi looked at him suspiciously. "I don't have designs on your body, if that's what you're thinking, Marshal," she denied almost too quickly. "Not that it's any of your business, mind you. But any man I join in bed won't be heading out at five in the morning to get aerated by whatever fool criminal happens to want to use him for target practice."

That woke him up. "I don't recall inviting you into my bed," Levi said tersely. "But just out of curiosity, what do you have against men who uphold law and order?"

"Everything, Hunter. Everything's in the minus column and nothing in the plus, as far as I'm concerned. Now, are you going to sit there all day jawing, or are you going to get on with this mission?"

Levi wasn't in the habit of dressing in front of a woman—at least not a woman who hadn't spent the night in his bed. Not that there had been so many of those, either, choosy as he was. But darned if Franzi DeLisle didn't have a way of making him forget he'd been raised a gentleman.

Acting deliberately, he slid one leg out from under the sheet and into his freshly laundered pants. Too bad for her if she didn't have sense enough to leave.

Franzi fought wild panic. "Law and order is an impossible dream, Marshal," she argued loudly, determined not to let him get to her. "I've learned over the years that all dreams are a waste of time."

Levi stood and turned away to button his jeans over the shorts he was darned thankful he'd decided to wear to bed. She irritated him, trying to sound so tough. "A hard philosophy from a woman who indulges in satin sheets. But go ahead with your charade," he growled, "if it makes you feel better to spit out 'Marshal' like it's a dirty word. It's a job I do, like you raise horses." Still half-asleep, he advanced on her. "Which way to the shower?"

He moved so fast Franzi's nose almost touched the dark thatch of hair covering his chest. She felt little fingers of heat pucker her skin. Lower lip clamped between her teeth, she let knocking knees carry her several steps down the hall, then pointed wordlessly to the bathroom door. She recovered enough to say, "I don't raise horses, Marshal. I raise mules."

He stopped abruptly.

Franzi loved besting him. She laughed. "I'm surprised you didn't hear about it in town. Folks brag that Jessup's the mule capital of the world. Usually talk gets around to their crazy mule lady."

Levi scowled. "You do have some horses, though—right? Since you're cross-breeding donkeys with horses to get your mules."

"The marshal gets a gold star," she said sarcastically. "So they do study the birds and bees in Utah."

A flush crawled up Levi's neck.

Franzi felt a bit—just a bit—contrite. Perhaps he hadn't deserved that. Perhaps she shouldn't assume that his opinions of women who raised mules were the same as those of the men around here. She offered an apology of sorts. "It's too early for sparring, Marshal. If you'll just get your butt in gear, we'll go take a look at those tracks."

Despite his reluctance, Levi gave in to the idea of her accompanying him. She was clearly a woman with a mind of her own. He again found himself watching the sway of her hips as she walked away, then strode into the bathroom and slammed the door. Once more she'd had the last word, and after he'd promised himself she wouldn't, too!

He had precious little trouble visualizing Ms. DeLisle matching wits with one of her mules. In fact, the poor beast might even have his sympathy. However, he, Levi Hunter, connoisseur of horseflesh, wouldn't be riding a mule today. Or any other day. The stubborn Ms. DeLisle could bank on that.

Her bathroom was as utilitarian as her bedroom. Levi slathered his face with shaving cream he'd found in the cabinet and thought about other willful females he knew. His mother, for one. Idly he wondered how she'd view Franzi. It was something to consider as he helped himself to a razor. His sisters, on the other hand, were all pretty traditional, and they'd married traditional men. Levi ran a hand over his smooth jaw, stepped under the shower and chuckled. Franzi DeLisle telling him to get his butt in gear would cause quite a stir in his family.

Restored to good humor, Levi collected his shirt and buttoned it as he went down the hall. Franzi intrigued him. If his mission had been less crucial, he'd have enjoyed exploring the interest she sparked.

He was still tucking his shirttail into his pants when he stopped in the kitchen to pick up his hat. Lisa was seated at the table, staring morosely into a cup of coffee.

"That stuff will rust your pipes," Levi teased. Though clearly pregnant, she reminded him of his youngest sister.

Glancing up, she frowned. "Franzi called Commissioner Parker. Before you came here, she wouldn't have had any part in this scheme." Lisa slumped in her chair and twisted a strand of straight dark hair around one finger.

Levi clipped the handcuffs to one of his belt loops. "Excuse me? Should I be participating or are you giving a monologue?"

"Things must be different in the city, Marshal."

Levi settled a battered Stetson on his head. "Sure. But I grew up in a town in Utah about the size of Jessup called Moab."

"Does Utah have any women sheriffs?" Lisa swished a spoon halfheartedly around in her cup.

Levi frowned, moving toward the door. "Yes, I know a few. Why? Are you planning a career in police work?"

"Are you nuts?" She glared at him. "Not me. Franzi!"

Levi laughed and pushed open the back door. "If that's what has you worried, young lady, you can relax. I think she'd rather walk barefoot over hot coals."

"Then why'd she call Daryl?" Lisa demanded.

Levi rolled his eyes. They'd come full circle. He shrugged. "I really have to go." He jerked his head toward the door. "Your...sister, is it?" he asked hesitantly, realizing he didn't know the women's relationship. "She's not a patient woman."

"Franzi shouldn't be going."

"You got that right," Levi agreed. "But she's all fired up about these tracks. Take my word for it, she'll be back by lunch. Oh, listen, thanks for washing my clothes. I feel almost human again. Now you lock the door when I leave, okay?" Because Lisa didn't look at all mollified, he added, "I meant what I said last night. Hunting Eilert isn't a job for a woman." Tipping his hat, he motioned once again to the lock, then left.

"I guess he'll find out Franzi isn't just *any* woman," Lisa muttered, dragging herself out of the chair to do his bidding.

Levi's boots crunched on gravel as he stepped off the porch. "What the hell?" he swore, eyeing the string of long-eared mules.

Franzi straightened from checking a loose girth buckle, returning his disdainful look across the animal's back.

"I see the shower didn't help. An hour not enough sleep for you, Hunter, or are you always surly before breakfast?" Giving one last yank on the load, Franzi pulled on a pair of soft kid gloves. She didn't look his way again until she'd gathered the reins of her mount and swung easily into the saddle. Gazing down at him was a mistake.

In the early-morning light, with his face cleanly shaven and dark hair curling against his black shirt collar, Levi Hunter was too male to suit her—much too male. And younger than she'd first thought. Early thirties she'd guess.

"Let's move it," she ordered, choking up on the reins and kicking the sides of her mule with her heels. The contradictory actions confused JoJo, the Mammoth Jack she was riding, and he almost smacked her in the face with a toss of his long ears.

Levi continued to stare at the second saddled mule. His hands rested loosely on his hips and his jaw tensed. "You don't actually intend for *me* to ride a mule? I mean, if *you* want to get calluses in unmentionable places, that's one thing. I don't, thank you very much."

"You'd rather walk?"

Levi removed then reset his hat, resting it firmly above his glowering brows. "Of course I wouldn't rather walk. Didn't we cover this earlier? If you breed mules, you obviously have horses." His voice rose along with his eyebrows. "Where do I go to saddle one?"

JoJo's ears twitched. Franzi flicked away a fly with the end of her reins. "You do much tracking in the Sierras?" Her voice was deceptively calm.

He tested the saddle with one hand and, finding it secure, gave a noncommittal grunt. "I know horses, Ms. Smarty Britches. Half my family raises quarter horses, the other half Arabians. Both breeds have normal ears and—"

Franzi interrupted. "That doesn't answer my question. We're talking the high Sierras, Hunter, not a Sunday rodeo or a beauty contest." Then, because she knew all about male egos, she softened her tone. "Up there—" she jerked a thumb toward the upper ridge of mountains "—you're going to hit trails so steep mountain goats avoid them. There'll be places the trail peters out altogether. If you're forced to go higher, you'll hit granite iced slick as glass from melting spring snows."

Her troubled gaze swept the distant snowcapped peaks. "I'm worried about Cricket, Hunter. If your man is stupid enough to take her up there..." She shook her head. "I can't even begin to tell you how many of those drop-offs end up as graveyards for horses—to say nothing of their riders." She looked down and met his eyes squarely. "Our Mountain Rescue teams ride mules, Hunter."

Levi scowled and pulled his hat lower. "What are these extra leather things hooked to the front and back of the saddle?"

She doused a smile. "Front one's a breastplate. The back one's called a crupper."

"Add a lot of unnecessary weight, don't they?"

Franzi shook her head. "Mules need the added support. They don't have the heavy withers of a horse." She leaned forward to stroke her mount's nose. "This is JoJo, and yours is Rebel."

"Figures," he grumbled. "Oh, well, I suppose... when in Rome..." He shrugged and gathered the reins, mounting swiftly with a skill and grace equal to hers. "That pack animal will slow me down. When we get where we're headed, I'll add a few things to these saddlebags and you can take the critter back with you." Half-standing in his stirrups, he tested their length. Finding it satisfactory, he turned to see why she hadn't delivered a smart comeback. She was already halfway across the clearing.

"Wait up," he called, but she had urged her mount into a trot and was well ahead. The rigid set of her back drew a grim smile. Maybe she was disappointed he'd given in so easily. But practical considerations had to outweigh aesthetics—and pride. Nudging the mule to a trot, Levi had to admit that the beast's gait wasn't nearly as bad as he'd expected.

He drew abreast of Franzi and shot her a look out of the corner of one eye. Her coppery hair was braided more tightly this morning. A real shame. In her bed last night he'd spent a moment picturing it loose and flowing over her satin pillow.

Abruptly he backed off and allowed her to ride ahead. Thoughts like that could get a man in trouble. Too soon, Levi realized that falling behind wasn't such a good idea, either. He watched her trim hips in their snug-fitting denim and felt something clench in his stomach. Something he should ignore.

Just then, his self-appointed guide turned to see why he'd dropped behind the pack animal. A rising sun bathed her creamy skin, turning it to molten gold.

Levi felt his breath lock. There was absolutely no denying that he found Franzi DeLisle an enigma. Right now, though, he desperately needed to concentrate on what he was going to say when it came time to send her back. And she *was* going back. Soon.

"Ready for breakfast?" Franzi met him with a sunny smile. She dug in her saddlebag and produced a plastic sack filled with sections of peeled orange.

Although he hesitated, Levi accepted the wedge she offered. Were all women nurturers? he wondered. Even tough ones? He knew about his sisters and Amanda, but somehow, Franzi hadn't seemed the type to cosset a man.

He savored the fruit and asked himself if he'd like being cosseted. Lately, he'd been thinking he might like to give it a try.

Franzi smiled again, and Levi decided he'd better get his mind off a subject that had no place here. Mules. Yes, they'd be a safe topic. "Looks to me like you have a good-size ranch," he observed. "Quite a spread for a woman to handle alone, isn't it?" But all at once it occurred to him that he might be assuming too much. After all, there had been signs of a man at the house.

"Men! You're all the same. Gage used to give me the same song and dance. I'll answer you the same as I did him. Why *not* a woman?"

Gage—the name had cropped up before. Levi's throat closed around the piece of orange. Ah, yes. Those were his things in the bathroom. His fingers tightened on the fruit, and he suddenly felt juice drip. Trying to seem casual, he wiped his hand across his clean jeans. "Does Gage have a last name?"

Franzi had just popped the final slice into her mouth. Her eyes met the marshal's over the tips of her fingers, then reining sharply to the left, she headed toward the grove of timber where she'd last sighted their intruder.

Hunter was asking about more than Gage's last name, she knew. Although she had little experience with the subtleties that passed between men and women, Franzi could tell by his tone that he was asking what her relationship with Gage was.

If the marshal didn't make her feel so...so disconnected, as if there was nothing holding her body together but strands of cooked spaghetti, she'd simply have told him Gage was her brother. But because he was a lawman—one who confused her, infuriated her and made her feel like a woman—she decided to answer only the question he'd asked.

She let him catch up, then without meeting his eyes, said, "His last name was DeLisle. Sheriff Gage DeLisle. We buried him a month ago."

"Oh. I see." Levi turned his face away and dropped back a pace.

Franzi felt awful. He didn't see—and yet, not for one minute, did she dare forget that he was walking death. A target looking for a loaded gun. No matter how he made her feel, there could be nothing between them. *Nothing!* Men like Hunter were wedded to their badges. And what about Amanda, the woman who'd been shot by Eilert? What was she to Hunter—and what was he to her?

Composing her features, Franzi pointed to a copse of trees and said briskly, "There, Marshal. The last look I got at our intruder, he was heading into the trees just about there."

Levi followed the direction of her finger, trying not to dwell on the fact that he was back to being called Marshal, and in sharp tones, yet. He had a few lingering questions—questions he didn't have the stomach to ask. Such as, how desperately had she loved Sheriff Gage to make her hate his entire profession so much?

Racing ahead, Franzi let out a whoop. "Here, Hunter. I've found his tracks."

Dismounting, Levi hurried to the spot where she was kneeling. A print was visible in the soft earth—it might have even been that of a horse's hoof—but mostly the area looked like a jumble of ridges and leaves. He couldn't be at all certain; he hadn't had any assignments outside of big cities for years.

"These are Cricket's tracks all right." Franzi pointed at the loamy soil. "That no-good . . . !" she exclaimed. "He hobbled my mare right here and he spied on us." She shivered and her eyes clouded. "Can't say how long he stayed, but I'll bet he saw you arrive."

Levi crouched beside her. He studied the flattened grass, the broken twigs and the dents. "You're sure?" Nothing in the network of indentations looked conclusive to him.

Franzi leapt to her feet. "Am I sure? Am I sure?" Twin spots of color rose in her cheeks. "Look, buster..." She tugged him up and dragged him over beneath the largest pine. "Cigarette butts. Four of them. And here." She went down on one knee and slapped the soil. "See the sharper dent in the left side of this print? He's loaded the pack mule unevenly. See this long mark? It shows Cricket's dragging her right rear leg. She just went through a mean delivery and has a little nerve damage. Dammit! Your man Eilert is much too heavy to be riding her!"

"You don't need to act tough for me, Ms. DeLisle."

Franzi drew back, narrowing her gaze. "Well, excuse me all to heck, Marshal. But when someone steals my best brood mare, it makes me mad." Her chin inched up a notch. "Maybe you should be toting a Bible, Marshal, instead of a badge."

Levi compressed his lips as he met the blaze in her eyes. "Maybe you should hightail it back to the ranch where you belong."

Franzi scanned his handsome features, looking for softness. What she saw was a man too much like her father. Except that he was probably looking at her and remembering Amanda again.

"It's very hard when you lose a...a..." She didn't know how to refer to Amanda. "Lover," she settled on at last.

"Yes," he agreed, his jaw tense. Of course she meant Gage. She must have loved him very much. Needing to change the subject, Levi said tersely, "So which way is Eilert headed?"

Franzi turned and vaulted into the saddle. "North. My guess is he hopes to lose you somewhere above the snow line. Let's go."

Levi grabbed JoJo's bridle. "Not we. Just me."

Franzi tried backing her mule away, but the marshal's grip was too strong. For several moments she stared into his implacable gray eyes, then she looked away and shrugged. "Eilert's got at least a two-hour head start." Tipping her face up to the sun, she ventured in a reasonable tone, "It's such a pretty morning. I'd consider it a treat to get away from the ranch for a few hours. Would you object if I rode along to the edge of my property—to make sure he didn't cut my fence?" Her smile was disarming.

Levi's fingers relaxed and Franzi's mule pulled free. He felt the orange wedges settle like lead sinkers in his stomach. He should heed the warning bells going off in his head, but what she said made sense. Enough sense, anyway, for Levi to find himself smiling back.

"Okay. You want to play hooky from mucking barns, far be it from me to stop you. Not one step beyond the fence, though," he cautioned. "I travel light. I'll take what I need from the pack mule and he goes back with you."

Franzi nodded agreeably. "The trail forks just beyond my property line. I'll tag along to that point—to make sure Eilert's still moving north."

Levi mounted, happy to hear she could be reasonable about some things. Maybe since her husband had been a sheriff, she understood more about danger than he'd given her credit for. Now if only that orange would quit playing handball in his stomach.

They rode for a few miles without talking, each under the spell of the warm day and the earthy scent of the fallow fields. Suddenly Levi broke the silence. "Is Lisa related to you?"

"What?" Franzi whipped her head around. "What makes you ask?"

"A question she threw at me this morning. She wanted to know if Utah had women sheriffs." Levi shook his head. "Said she was inquiring on your behalf. I think it's pretty clear how you feel."

Franzi's brows knit. "How did you two get onto that subject?"

Levi covered a yawn. "I can't remember exactly how the conversation started. She might have asked about my work or something."

"I'm curious, too. Do you do much fieldwork?" Franzi's eyes narrowed. "And don't you guys who keep the peace in the concrete jungle wear guns?"

He touched the middle of his back, near his belt. "I have one. I just don't flaunt it."

Franzi ran a hand over her tooled leather scabbard. "I like mine handy. Alone on the range, a woman can't be too careful."

Levi's lips tightened. "I've never known a problem yet that's been solved by a citizen wearing a gun. Nor am I absolutely convinced we're better off with every cop carrying one. It's too easy for the wrong people to get hurt."

"Yes, well . . ." She paused. "Gage said that with a gun, a person at least has a fifty-fifty chance. Unless maybe that was Gage's warped sense of humor."

"I don't have a sense of humor when it comes to guns."

He'd spoken with such finality that silence fell between them again. Then, out of the blue, Franzi asked, "Did Amanda like the city?"

He looked up, surprised by her question. "At one time," he admitted reluctantly, "I thought she would. Instead, she chose to marry my best friend and be a farm wife." His voice thinned and faded. He might have said more had Franzi not reined in and gone stock-still.

"What is it?" he asked. "Why are you stopping? Is something wrong?"

"Wrong?" Franzi gaped at him. "I thought you and Amanda..." She closed her mouth, then opened it and burst out, "If you and Amanda weren't... you know..." She shrugged and gave it up. "Why isn't your best friend the one risking his life to run Eilert to ground?"

Levi removed his hat and raked a hand through his hair. "You and Lisa *must* be related," he muttered. "She talks in riddles, too." He supposed he might as well tell her the story. If she was anything like his sisters, she wouldn't let up until he had, anyway.

He began slowly, "The three of us, Adam, Amanda and I, were inseparable as kids and on into high school." A sheepish grin flashed in the sun. "Would it sound too conceited if I said I always assumed Amanda loved me best?"

Franzi didn't smile back, nor did she comment.

"Well, I did," he said with a small shrug. "I left for college expecting her to wait. Adam bought the horse ranch he'd always dreamed of owning. I came home on summer break to find myself best man at their wedding." He resettled his hat over his eyes and said gruffly, "Bringing in Popeye is the best I can do for either of them now."

Damn the man. Franzi tore her gaze away. Once again Levi Hunter had her sympathy when she didn't want to give it. Oh, she knew all about these altruistic missions. Hadn't her father...? Well, no matter. Something else she knew—when the job got too personal, the man wearing a badge threw caution to the wind. Which was downright dangerous.

"I didn't mean to open old wounds," she said. "What you do, and why, is your business, Hunter." Whether he admitted it or not, Levi Hunter still carried a torch for Amanda. *Love,* she snorted inwardly, *It makes good men careless.*

Levi watched desolation chase the sunlight from her eyes. He wouldn't have minded hearing something about her life, too, but not if it caused her more pain. "Hey," he chided, "all this stuff is too weighty for such a nice day." He smiled grimly. "I'll get Popeye. I'm smarter than he is."

"Yeah, that's what they all say." Touching her heels to her mule, Franzi galloped ahead.

Less than five hundred yards up the hill, she came to the barbed wire. It marked the end of her property and it was where the trail split. Pointing casually, she reined in well behind the wire. Let him be Amanda's dead hero. Why should she risk caring?

Levi climbed down from Rebel and took a few things from the pack mule to add to his saddlebags. "So this is goodbye," he said firmly, as he secured the bags behind his saddle.

"You'd better come back in one piece, Hunter," she said in a fierce voice, unable to maintain her pretense of not caring. "You have one of my best mules, you know, and Eilert has my favorite mare."

Levi laughed. "Your concern is touching." He placed a hand over his heart. "Almost more than a man can take. Shall we say so long, then? Is that better?"

She scowled, snatched up the lead line to the pack jenny and backed JoJo away.

"I must say you surprise me," he said. "I expected I'd have to hog-tie you and send you back slung over that mule."

"You and what army?" She gave him a saucy toss of her head. "Maybe I've just learned to *choose* my battles."

"Good thing." Levi left her and rode through the gate, wondering why he didn't feel better about having the last word this time.

Franzi watched him approach the divide and promptly take the wrong fork. It was evident the lawman from the concrete jungle lacked skill as a tracker. "Hunter," she called, after some serious consideration, "if you have a compass in your little bag of tricks, I suggest you break it out. I'm afraid you have the north end of your mule heading south. Eilert's tracks lead in the other direction."

Levi stopped, practically causing Rebel to land on his haunches. Dismounting, he led the mule back to the Y and stared down at the ground.

Franzi edged JoJo through the fence. She climbed down and pointed to a network of prints. "Tracks—Cricket's first, followed by the pack-jenny." JoJo pulled at his reins and bugled.

Levi scowled. "Do they make gross noises like that often?"

Franzi ignored him. "I'd guess Eilert's still a couple of hours ahead of you. And Cricket's limp is worse. Do you hear what I'm saying, Marshal?"

Levi pretended to study the faint marks, which might as well have been chicken tracks for all the sense he made of them. He fought down an urge to admit he'd been the only Boy Scout in Moab who'd missed getting a much-coveted badge after failing miserably to identify a bear track. A bear track, his sister Laura still delighted in telling anyone who would listen, the size of a barn door. "Our technical manuals do cover tracking," he said, wondering if he was being foolish in insisting she go back, after all.

But no. He'd done a little tracking—about ten years ago, true—but the skill would come back with practice. Wouldn't it? In any event, he refused to put her life in danger. "Two hours, you say? Well—" he attempted a laugh "—that ought to put me back at your ranch around suppertime, right?"

His little-boy swagger caught Franzi off guard.

"Are you a good cook, DeLisle?" He nudged her, the question bordering on cocky. "If so, set an extra place for dinner, and tell Deputy Lee to throw a double lock on his jail. I'll be bringing him a guest tonight."

Franzi's stomach bottomed out. When the marshal teased in that lazy, sexy drawl, it curled her toes right inside her sturdy leather boots. And yet something about his audacity irked her. "Dinner's at six, Hunter. Get there in time to wash up."

"I like my steak rare." Levi was forced to raise his voice, since she'd lost no time in taking herself and her mules back across the divide.

"I might have guessed, Hunter. You macho types all have the same tastes. Gage liked his meat red in the middle, too."

Levi's smile became a scowl.

Franzi could hardly miss it, and she worried her lower lip guiltily. Making up her mind, she called in a low voice, "Something else, Hunter. Gage DeLisle was my brother."

Speechless, Levi stared. "Hey, wait!" he shouted, as she whirled and trotted down the trail in a cloud of dust. Soon, even the steady clop-clop of her mule's hooves had dwindled away.

He thumbed his hat to a rakish angle and let out a whoop. This time, he didn't mind that she'd had the last word; he didn't mind at all. Still smiling, he rode up the trail. When he reached the first ridge of trees, the noonday sun was doing its level best to send weak rays through a thick canopy of pine branches. Carefully he calculated the number of hours left until dinner and basked for a time in the warm glow of anticipation.

The glow stayed with him for most of the afternoon. Until the going got really rough and the terrain all began to look the same and the sun showed every sign of sinking in the west—which at least allowed him to identify which way was west.

Levi couldn't remember exactly when he'd given up the idea of sharing dinner with Franzi DeLisle, but it had been a while back. And now he was forced to deal with the fact that he hadn't a clue where on her stupid mountain he was. More than once he wished pride hadn't stood in the way of asking her more about these trails. Especially after the sun had strayed behind a snowy peak and he lost sight of *any* tracks—his own, as well as Eilert's. And as if that wasn't bad enough, Levi suddenly had an uneasy feeling he'd seen that squat, funny-looking tree in front of him before.

How long, if at all, would Franzi wait dinner for him? he wondered dismally. Would she worry? He weighed the possibility. Not likely. Dismissing the idea as easily as it had come, he checked his watch. Almost six-thirty. He smoothed a hand down the plodding mule's neck and envisioned Franzi DeLisle smugly eating without him.

As evening shadows danced eerily across his path, he decided to look for a campsite. His backside was numb and his mind drifting. All at once he rounded a sharp turn where a stiff breeze blowing from the north carried a faint trace of wood smoke.

He reined in fast. "Eilert!" The killer's name escaped his cold lips. All thoughts of Franzi suddenly metamorphosed into deadly visions of Mandy's attacker.

Dismounting with some difficulty, thanks to his long hours in the saddle, Levi took care to avoid the creaking of leather. Quietly he looped Rebel's reins around a rotting stump and painstakingly began to sneak up the side hill.

Dusk lengthened. Fortunately for Levi, the moon was slow to rise. He passed a stand of timber and was just able to make out the shadowy rump of a tethered animal. Good. He had the element of surprise. Soon he drew close to a wildly flickering camp fire, sheltered by a ring of granite boulders. Leaping flames threw long, grotesque shadows of his quarry across a sheer canyon wall. He had Eilert boxed in.

Levi calculated how long it would take the man to reach the rifle leaning negligently against a downed log. Allowing for the distance, he crouched, then dived.

Even as he flew through the air, his target shifted. Unable to correct himself midair, Levi landed hard on his shoulder. His thirty-eight went flying. Quickly he tucked and rolled, expecting to come up meeting the cold steel of

Eilert's gun. He had few regrets in his life, yet the ones he had all flashed through his mind—and they included missing dinner with Franzi DeLisle.

As his eyelids slowly lifted, he was greeted by the sight of her, calm as you please, spearing a juicy steak from an iron grate nestled deep in the flames. The long-handled fork she used to slap the meat onto the plate was what he'd taken for Eilert's rifle.

"Your steak is quite well-done, Hunter," she said evenly. "What took you so long?"

CHAPTER FOUR

"WHAT IN BLAZES do you think you're doing?" Levi shouted, massaging his sore shoulder. His fury ran white-hot.

"Fixing dinner, Marshal." Her calm voice carried the barest hint of amusement. "You have a choice of biscuits or beans with your steak—or if you're really hungry after stumbling around so long out on the trail, I'll give you both."

Tight-lipped, Levi stood, retrieved his hat and gun and dusted off his pants. He counted slowly to ten as he clamped down on his temper. "I thought you were Eilert," he said in a voice rough with feeling. "Do you know how close I came to hurting you?"

"Really?" Franzi glanced at the dirty, snub-nosed gun. But it was his unfamiliar tone that convinced her to stifle the remainder of her retort. She offered him the plate. "Eilert's still going north," she said mildly. "He's gained about half an hour on us, but he's bedded down for the night. Take a load off, Marshal. Eat before your meal gets cold."

"Us?" Levi barely managed to keep his tone civil. "How do you know so much about Eilert's activity? I sent you back to the ranch!"

"I've been keeping tabs on him with high-powered binoculars."

"Did you pack me binoculars?"

"Doesn't a federal marshal carry his own? Anyway, Eilert's well across the gorge. He won't see my fire, if that's what has you worried."

"*You're* what has me worried, lady. I thought you were safe at home."

Franzi lifted her chin stubbornly and urged the plate toward him again.

Levi decided there was little point in arguing with her. She was alive and that was what counted. Alive and well, he had to admit. He accepted the steak and the utensils she held out. With knees still somewhat rubbery, he flopped down on a fallen log. He had to admit the aroma alone made his mouth water. The beans she dished up were dark with molasses the way he liked them, and the biscuits looked as light and fluffy as his mother's.

"Thanks," he muttered, belatedly remembering his manners. "But we'll finish this discussion, I promise you." He spared his gun a glance and made a mental note to clean it later. His scowl remained ferocious.

Franzi paid little heed to his temper. "I'll just go take care of Rebel while my steak cooks," she said, replacing the narrow grate over the small fire. "You should rest him as much as possible. Tomorrow we'll be pushing hard to make up for lost time."

Levi stopped with a bite halfway to his mouth. He set his plate aside and stood, wondering how she could've made him mad enough to forget his mule. But he had only to look at her slender body to know. His stomach knotted just thinking about what could have happened to her, had she stumbled on Eilert.

"*We* aren't going anywhere tomorrow," he said, stabbing a finger in the air. "Come daylight, *you'll* make tracks for the ranch and *I* will continue after Eilert. And I don't need you doing my chores, either," he grumbled. "I'll go tend to Rebel."

"Suit yourself." She shrugged. "If you prefer cold steak, it's fine with me. Mine needs at least five minutes to be the way I like it. In the interests of fairness, I was going to suggest you clean up." She wrinkled her nose. "Unless of course you consider that women's work."

Ignoring what he viewed as unwarranted sarcasm, Levi dropped back to the log and retrieved his plate. She'd annoyed him quite enough for one day. "You'll find Rebel off to the left of the trail about three hundred yards down the hill. Don't fall down a ravine in the dark. I can't manage two steaks."

Franzi slanted him a dark look. She wasn't sure she liked his giving back as good as he got. Gage had always tried to goad her, but he was family. Maybe that was it—the marshal reminded her of her brother. Heaven forbid! She grimaced as she walked away. Although it might explain the obsession she had with keeping him safe, she hardly thought the turmoil in the pit of her stomach could be classed as a sisterly feeling. Nor could this catch in her breath.

Burying her hands in her jacket pockets, Franzi trudged down the trail. Gage's badge felt cold against her fingers. What had she thought to accomplish by agreeing with Daryl to fill Gage's shoes, even temporarily? Deep down she knew—had known before she left home this morning. Hunter was a lawman. And lawmen never listened to reason. But that didn't mean she could stand by and watch him die.

Franzi jerked her hand out of her pocket. Hadn't she also known how very difficult it was to save a lawman bent on dying? Sooner or later they all got to thinking they were indestructible. Sooner or later they all tempted fate—and lost.

Did Hunter really think he'd be eating steak tonight if she'd been Eilert? Probably. He was that arrogant.

Rebel brayed and Franzi patted his nose. Mules, now, lived a good long time. Men, at least the ones she'd known, didn't fare so well. Yet, Levi Hunter wasn't going to become a statistic in Alano County if she could help it.

Collecting his animal and stopping for the other two she'd tethered earlier, an even more determined Franzi headed back to camp.

Levi looked up as she led their mules into the thin circle of light. The knot in his stomach relaxed. "Took you long enough," he complained, watching her capable hands loosen Rebel's saddle and drop it to the ground. "Your steak's looking black around the edges."

"It's dark out there, Hunter, and I didn't want to step off a cliff and make your day." She gave a saucy flip of her braid. "Besides, charcoal keeps my teeth white."

Levi slammed his nearly empty plate down and got to his feet. "I'll finish up with the animals. You eat. A full stomach does wonders for a wicked tongue. We can settle our differences later."

"Food hasn't seemed to help *your* disposition." Franzi glanced up then and caught him rubbing his backside with both hands. She laughed and watched him quickly pretend nothing was wrong. "Sore, Marshal?" she teased. "Surely not you—the man who demanded a horse? Why, compared to a horse, Rebel's gait is gentle as a rocking chair."

Levi smiled ruefully. "Not quite that gentle." He passed a hand over his back pockets again. "And you're discounting aesthetics. A trim, pretty horse makes a man feel good about riding. Mules are powerful ugly."

"They are not. They have character." Franzi made a face at him. "Anyhow, you'd have had an hour less saddle time if you hadn't ridden in circles." Tossing him the lead rope to her pack jenny, she slipped past him and snatched up her steak.

The air all but crackled with static. Franzi had never experienced anything like it in her life. She felt his unusual gray eyes bore through her. As nonchalantly as she could, she buttered her biscuit and set the plate on a rock to stay warm while she started a pot of coffee. She returned to her meal and tried to focus on problems at the ranch. Difficult though they might be, problems there were infinitely less threatening than thinking about the charge that had passed between Hunter and herself a moment ago. "Why don't you yell at me now and get it over with?" she finally said, reluctant to wait for the confrontation she knew was coming.

"Eat first. I'd hate to spoil your dinner," he said, leading the mules away.

"Why do I feel like the condemned being allowed one last meal?"

He turned and saw her stick out her tongue.

She blushed.

"I didn't mean for you to take it that way. Oh, and thanks—the food was great."

Franzi toyed with her beans. None of the DeLisle men ever gave compliments or discussed feelings. Not hers or theirs. After her mother died, she'd been treated the same as Gage. She often wondered how life would have been if her father had remarried. Deep in her musing, Franzi tried imagining the kind of woman who would appeal to a lawman. Amanda's kind, obviously. At least, Hunter's voice took on a certain reverence every time her name surfaced.

Franzi's thoughts swung back to the problems at her ranch—as she stared blankly into the crackling flames of the fire. Her main barn needed a new roof this year. Thinking of barns didn't leave lumps in her stomach.

Levi sauntered back into the ring of firelight and stopped across from her. "You know, I'd almost forgotten how much time it takes to bed down animals." He stretched. "Not only time, but energy."

She watched the play of his thigh muscles beneath the worn denim and almost choked on a biscuit. "Uh...you probably haven't dealt with this altitude before," she said around a full mouth. "Our thinner air saps a person's strength." Franzi knew she was babbling. If only he'd quit doing calisthenics in front of her nose! She swallowed to clear her throat and tried again. "I guess you didn't stop to consider how steadily you've been climbing. That's why riding mules up here makes better sense. They don't get winded like horses." She set her plate aside and avoided looking at him.

"Interesting facts you keep throwing my way about mules," Levi drawled, taking a seat on the opposite log. "However, I'll admit I acted like an equine snob this morning at your ranch. It's just that in southern Utah, where I grew up, it's common to measure a man's worth by the bloodline of his horses."

"Bloodline is important to me, too," she said, steepling her fingers. "I'm trying to perfect a mule with speed, stamina and looks."

"Tall order. With long ears and knobby knees, I tell you they're hopeless. Now you take a good quarter horse—"

"You *are* a snob, Hunter." Franzi watched the coffeepot bubble. "You could stand some mellowing." Getting up, she dug around in her pack and pulled out two battered tin mugs and a small silver flask.

"Ahh!" she murmured, cracking the cap and closing her eyes. "This is a good old DeLisle tradition. Perfect for topping off the first night on the trail—coffee with a little nudge." Deftly she measured a shot into each cup, then filled them to the brim with dark brew. "Just to prove I don't hold grudges—here, Hunter, I'll share my Irish whiskey." Franzi stretched an arm across the fire. "Nights up here get damned cold. This takes the edge off."

He left her more or less hanging in midair and frowned up at the stars winking overhead. "How cold is damned cold? Whiskey takes the edge off reflexes too, you know."

Franzi pulled back her arm and set down his mug, then deliberately took a hefty swallow from the other. She ran her tongue over her lips and savored the stinging warmth. "When the fire goes out, it'll get cold as a polar bear's, uh...'' She coughed, quickly correcting the ending Gage generally attached to that particular saying. "A polar bear's tail. In city lingo, that means damned cold," she added bluntly.

"This city dweller has seen cigarettes, whiskey...and wild, wild women ruin more than one good agent on a chase."

"Well, you aren't my keeper, Hunter, or my conscience."

"Amen to that, DeLisle." Levi rose. "If I was, you could bet your boots you'd be home snuggled between those satin sheets." Bending, he picked up his plate and hers.

Franzi fought against the wave of heat clawing its way up her neck. She glanced up belatedly. "What are you doing now? Can't you sit still?"

Levi's lips curved upward. "Cleaning up, milady. I believe that was a condition of being fed. When I finish this chore, I'll turn in. You can roll out of bed and head home any time the spirit moves you, but I intend to be on Eilert's trail at dawn."

"If you recognize his trail," Franzi bit back. "I swear—you sure know how to ruin a tradition." Glaring, she stood and poured his whiskey-coffee and the remaining dregs of her own over the fire.

Steam sizzled between them. "I'll wash my own dishes," she informed him. "Lord knows I wouldn't want you to demean yourself." She grabbed one of the enameled plates he was holding.

"Temper, temper," he admonished as she wrested it away. But when the force landed her on her rump, he instantly turned solicitous. "Are you okay? You didn't hurt yourself, did you?" He knelt beside her, and she was shocked by the genuine concern in his voice.

She scrambled up. "Only my pride, Hunter, only my pride."

He picked up the cups and watched her march off to the edge of the campsite where she scraped her meat scraps from the plate behind a granite boulder. When Levi sauntered in her direction, she decided to come back later to bury them. Certain he wouldn't follow her into the darkness, she yelled over her shoulder, "Maybe I'll work on my temper when you stop using that holier-than-thou tone, Hunter." Kneeling beside the stream that bubbled with icy clarity from beneath a granite boulder, she swished the plate furiously.

Levi stood there a moment, feeling badly about baiting her. She couldn't possibly know how evil Eilert was, and she had cared enough to chase him down and feed him. Not that he'd let her get in the way of danger, but he needn't have acted so high-handed.

"Here, let me do that," he said gruffly, stepping up behind her and reaching down to clasp her elbow. "There's an unwritten rule in my mother's house—the cook never does the dishes."

Startled to find him so close, Franzi let herself be pulled erect. His eyes seemed softer in the moonlight, and the feelings she'd been avoiding began to dance in her stomach. But suddenly the same moonlight that made him human glinted off the pocket that held his badge. And Franzi remembered.

She hated the fact that his badge changed everything. But it did. And she needed to protect her heart. "A lawman with dishpan hands," she scoffed, making a show of disengaging her arm. "I wonder about you, Hunter. Whiskey is apparently taboo. And cigarettes... Well, I won't go into that. Do you city cops do anything manly, I wonder?"

The metal cups slid through Levi's fingers and clattered against a slab of granite, followed by the plates he swatted from her hand.

Although she'd had little experience recognizing a man's desire, Franzi knew male fury when she saw it. Stepping back, she slipped on a slick rock and almost landed in the stream.

He reached out, wrapped both hands around her upper arms and yanked her forward.

She hit a solid six-foot wall of muscle and felt the breath go out of her. "Now, Hunter," she squeaked, "no need to get physical." But then Franzi looked up and got lost in gray eyes that turned from flint to wispy smoke in less than a heartbeat. Fascination soon turned to panic as the heat from his body melted the starch in her knees.

She expected him to bluster about women, or maybe raise his voice in defense of his manhood, the way Gage and his friends did when she bested them—but there was absolutely nothing in Franzi's past to prepare her for the swift hard way Levi's lips descended on hers.

Shocked, she struggled. Almost immediately her knees gave way, and she was forced to rely on the strength of his arms to keep from falling. Quite without volition, her fingers curled into the front of his shirt and her body swayed against his hard contours.

Levi began withdrawing the instant she struggled. First and foremost, he was a man of principle. He'd never kissed a woman against her will, and he didn't intend to start with one who barely knew she was a woman. But she slid so rapidly from resistance into pliancy his senses reacted automatically, and his fingers strayed from her arms to curve around her slender back. A back that displayed a tantalizing mix of tensile strength and womanly softness. All of those truths hit just as the heavenly scent of honeysuckle engulfed him....

She made a soft sound in her throat. Levi felt his control slip altogether. He relinquished her lips only when forced to take in air.

Her inviting mouth followed, begging for more.

He thought then that a man could live without oxygen. Capturing the lushness of her lips a second time, he couldn't think. Not when he felt closer to drowning.

She was so innocent. The thought flew across his mind. It was only for a split second, but that was time enough for Levi to comprehend that they were both being consumed by emotions he couldn't allow. Not while Eilert was still at large. Not when he knew what had happened to Mandy—what could happen to Franzi in the wink of an eye.

Heedless of his sudden withdrawal, Franzi continued to float in sensations outside of time. Until the moment he stepped back and she stumbled, she probably couldn't have said her own name to save her life.

Cool air filtered between them, making her blink up into Hunter's steely eyes. For a moment she honestly couldn't imagine why she was kissing him—a lawman. Then understanding intruded, and waves of shame washed over her, Whirling away from him, she faced the stream and gulped in great draughts of air.

He saw that she was having a hard time dealing with the unfamiliar effects of passion and stayed back to give her space. Not that he didn't want to explore further where it could lead, but he knew adrenaline tended to heighten emotions. And this was neither the time nor the place.

Franzi covered her cheeks with her palms, analyzing a kiss that was decidedly different from the chaste ones she'd shared with the braver of Gage's friends. The men of Jessup she hadn't scared off had generally been less than brave in the face of so many DeLisle badges. So why, when she'd given up any hope of finding romance with one of the local ranchers, did she have to discover the whole stomach-rocking, head-spinning experience now? With this man?

Levi decided she'd had enough time. Hesitantly he touched her shoulder.

"Don't." She shook off his warm fingers. She strove to resurrect the barriers she'd erected so carefully around her heart at the passing of each DeLisle. "If you were trying to prove you're no preacher's son, Hunter, you've made your point. Please, leave me alone."

Remorse tore through him, and he dropped his hand. "But I am," he said quietly, "more or less, anyway. I'm a bishop's son. Believe it or not," he added with a sigh, "I once gave serious thought to following in my father's footsteps."

Franzi's first instinct was to flee. But once his strange statement was out, curiosity gripped her. "Why didn't you? Do something safer, I mean?" she stammered, facing him directly. So many times she had wondered why the DeLisle men felt driven to wear a badge when they might easily have worked the land. Now here was a man who claimed he, too, had made a conscious choice. What had possessed him? She held her breath, waiting—hoping—for some magical answer that would make it all clear to her.

Levi's jaw tensed. How could she stand there asking about mundane things like careers? How could she brush off what they'd just shared as if it had never happened? For a moment, he considered grabbing her and kissing her again—except that wasn't his style. And the way the moonlight played across her pale cheeks, she looked as if she might shatter if he did.

He cleared his throat and waited until he had a grip on his emotions. "I suppose it's simple, really," he murmured. "I was in high school. You know, a time when a person's at a real crossroads in life. My father—a devout man, a wonderful father—went on a routine trip to town and took a bullet meant for a bank clerk. His killer was never caught. It made me angry. Too angry to think about counseling others in forgiveness. My mother suggested I find a better way to resolve my anger and still serve humanity. We hit upon law enforcement."

Something twisted in Franzi's chest. Her heart plunging to her toes in all likelihood. If he hadn't already gained her sympathy with Amanda's tale, this would have done the trick. "Undoubtedly your mother meant well, Hunter," she whispered, "but if I had a son, law enforcement is the last place I'd direct him. It's too risky. There are so many more demons to fight, and they're much better armed."

Levi could almost taste her bitterness. Strangely, he understood. "I'm sorry you lost your brother, Franzi. But all of life is a risk. My father proved as much. Someday it won't hurt so much. You'll see." He thought he probably ought to apologize for kissing her, too, since she hadn't exactly been offering an invitation. Somehow, though, he couldn't quite bring himself to express regret about that.

Franzi crossed her arms over her breasts. "I don't suppose you're sorry enough to give up this chase and let the guys in San Francisco worry about Eilert, are you?"

"Eilert is my responsibility," he said stiffly. "And you look like you're freezing. I suggest we both put this... unfortunate incident behind us, and you get back to the fire. I'll finish the dishes, while you figure out where you'd like me to throw my bedroll."

Franzi drew herself up as though he'd slapped her. It was his choice of words—"unfortunate incident," indeed—that got to her. "As far as I'm concerned, Hunter, you can throw it into the next county." She stalked away without another glance.

The camp fire remained cheerful, even if Franzi was not. She settled herself on a log and stared broodingly into the bed of glowing coals. Coals no hotter than her red face, she was sure.

She listened with half an ear to the sounds of Levi finishing chores. Chores she should be sharing. It had only been a simple kiss, for goodness' sake. She had to admit she'd actually found it pleasant. No, more than pleasant. And it offended her to think hers had disappointed him.

Melancholy set in and the new cup of coffee she'd poured grew cold. She tossed the muddy liquid over her shoulder and poured another—leaving the Irish out. Not, she told herself, because Hunter disapproved, but because she didn't have the energy to get up to retrieve the flask.

Beyond the firelight, one of the mules brayed. Franzi strained to hear. It sounded like JoJo. It was rare for him to make any noise on a trail ride. She listened carefully for other unusual sounds.

Levi moved back into the circle of light carrying a neat stack of clean dishes. They rattled and Franzi motioned for him to be quiet. "What's up?" he asked, his brow furrowing to match hers.

"I don't know," she murmured. "Maybe nothing. The animals seem a little restless. Could be a timber wolf, although normally they're higher up. Think I'll put another log on the fire and recheck the hobbles."

He put the dishes in her lap. "You stick close to the fire. I'll go take a look around."

"Careful, Hunter. You wouldn't want to spoil me now, would you? Or are you just hoping it might be Eilert? Well, you're wasting your time. He's way ahead of us, and he knows he's got the lead. But tomorrow, when the trail narrows and gets steep, he'll be traveling blind. From then on, it won't be so easy for him."

Levi battled annoyance. "You think because you lived with a sheriff that qualifies you as an expert?"

Franzi's temper flared. "Not *a* sheriff, Hunter. *Three* sheriffs." She set her cup aside and held up three fingers. "My father, my uncle—" she paused "—and G-Gage."

Levi's gaze narrowed. "Three? So how come you're ranching alone?"

She avoided his eyes and stripped branches from a good-size limb.

"Did you hear me?" he asked, walking over to pick up an entire log and placing it on the fire. "Where are the others?"

"I heard you. Look, dammit..." She jumped to her feet and jammed both hands into her pockets, then turned to stare out into the night. "I don't want to talk about this. If you aren't going to check the tethers, I'll do it."

Levi wasn't satisfied, but he'd seen enough to know Franzi's eyes were shadowed by grief. Against his better judgment, he pulled back. "If you roll out the sleeping bags, I'll go bring the animals into the clearing behind us. Any wolf trying to get them would have to pass our fire first."

"That's good. Wolves don't like fire." Her shoulders relaxed visibly. She offered a tentative smile. "It was probably nothing, Hunter. JoJo seems to have settled down." She shrugged. "On the other hand, we had a long winter and some late snows up here this spring. Wolves and coyotes might be lean. If we burn the fire all night, will you have trouble sleeping?"

Levi grinned. "Not me! I'm having trouble staying awake."

"I warned you about thinner air, didn't I?"

Even though her low chuckle was little more than a ripple of sound, it sent a burst of excitement through his body. Fortunately a log fell just then in a hail of sparks. Leaving her to contain the blaze, he made good his escape.

On returning to camp after moving the mules, Levi was relieved to find Franzi already snug in her sleeping bag, with only her bright hair showing. In spite of the enticing way it gleamed in the firelight, he found he was able to carry on a normal conversation. "You know, when you said it would get cold, I'll admit I thought you were stretching the truth," he said dryly. "Now my fingers are so numb I can hardly unzip my sleeping bag."

"I don't believe it, Hunter. A compliment at long last." She raised herself on one elbow and yawned. "In that case, I'll give you another piece of free advice. Strip down to your underwear before you climb into bed. Keep your pants and shirt inside the bag and then cover the whole thing with those two saddle blankets I left out. Maybe you won't look like an icicle in the morning."

"That's two pieces of advice, DeLisle. If only one is free, which one is going to cost me, and how much?" Levi sat on a nearby log and yanked off first one boot, then the other. "Or could it be," he murmured, pausing to wink at her, "that voyeurism is yet another of the lady's vices?"

Franzi snorted and rolled over, presenting him with her back. Above the snap and pop of the fire he'd just stoked, she heard him shedding his jacket. Next, the long zipper of his sleeping bag grated. After a few moments of silence, she knew he hadn't taken her advice.

Oh well. A woman could only do so much. Let him suffer. Sleeping in clothes was a common mistake of weekend campers at this time of year. Most of the people who came on her treks didn't know that their body temperature would remain higher if they were covered with no more than the lightly insulated fabric of the bag. But they, at least, tended to do as she suggested.

Franzi listened to Levi's even breathing for several minutes. Perhaps she shouldn't grumble about obstinacy, what with all those little falsehoods of her own. Over the snapping of the fire, she called softly, "Hunter, I have another confession."

"Really?" His skepticism floated on the crisp air.

"Yes, really," she mimicked, flopping over on her back to scowl up at the glittering stars. He had a way of making things so difficult. "I don't smoke," she admitted without preamble. "I quit more than two years ago."

Levi smiled and raised his head to get a look at her around the fire. Last night, sleeping in her bed, he'd suspected as much. Tonight, after kissing her, he knew for sure. "No lie?"

"No lie!" Franzi curled into her bag, satisfied she'd cleared a portion of her conscience. "I'm not a voyeur, either," she added, as lethargy stole over her—even though she was pretty certain that particular accusation had been made in jest.

Ten or fifteen minutes passed in silence. Franzi was just drifting off when suddenly she heard discreet scuffling noises coming from Hunter's bag. She clamped a hand over her mouth to keep from laughing aloud. It took him a while to process information, but once it sank in, he wasn't above taking a woman's advice. She indulged in a tiny bit of private gloating before she let sleep win.

Levi lay awake for some time marveling at her ability to drop off, especially considering the fact that Eilert was somewhere in the vicinity. Of course, she didn't know firsthand about Popeye's inhuman cruelty. To keep from remembering, he sought out the Big Dipper and the North Star. The exercise would keep him awake, in case she needed protecting. There were no two ways about it—tomorrow he'd send her home.

He tugged the blankets higher and tried to predict her reaction. She wouldn't like it one bit. He stifled a yawn. In the morning, come hell or high water, he was definitely having the last word.

A SCREAM, ALMOST HUMAN, catapulted both sleepers from deep slumber. The fire had burned low, and the moon, nearly hidden behind a distant ridge, shed little light.

Franzi's heart thumped loudly. She could feel her breath quicken in the frosty air.

"What was that?" Levi's rough whisper sounded groggy with sleep.

"Shh," she hissed impatiently, but relented once she remembered he was from the city. "It's a mountain cat," she said softly.

The scream came again. Much closer this time.

"A lynx?" Levi asked, his teeth chattering from the cold.

"Bigger. More like a cougar, I think."

Levi could hear faint scraping noises coming from somewhere between Franzi and the stream. In the narrow space behind them, the mules began to bray.

As silently as possible, Levi shrugged into his shirt and pants. Reaching out, he added some small twigs to the smoldering coals, then held his breath until they flared, expanding the circle of light.

"I can see him, Hunter," Franzi murmured. "He's just a stone's throw away eating my leftover steak." She swore under her breath. "Of all people, I should know to wrap and bury my scraps."

Levi added a larger piece of wood to the fire and quickly tugged on his stiff boots. "Quit worrying about what you should have done and come over here. Cats don't like fire any more than wolves do."

Franzi could see that the cougar had just about polished off the scraps. She calmly managed to wriggle into her pants in spite of the confining folds of the thick down bag and was already edging into her shirtsleeves when the cat lifted his head. His great golden eyes glinted in the firelight. He was gaunt from a long winter. Instinct told her the steak had only whetted his appetite.

She tried to shed her sleeping bag, but found the tail of her shirt caught firmly in the teeth of the metal zipper. She couldn't move.

"What's keeping you, DeLisle?" Levi commanded. "Hurry up!"

The cat leapt to a boulder above her head and snarled. She worked to keep the panic from her voice, but failed. "I'm stuck, Hunter!"

"Stuck!" He crept around the fire toward her just as the cat sailed through the air.

Franzi's scream ripped a jagged hole in his heart and his knees turned to jelly. Without thinking, he snatched the burning branch from the blaze and flew toward the beast, brandishing it like a sword.

"Are you crazy, Hunter?" He heard her gasp. "Get your gun!"

"Can't. Save your breath. I didn't clean it." Lunging again, he drove the cat back to the rocky ledge.

"Then get mine," she begged. "It's in the scabbard."

"No time," he muttered, as the cat hissed and flattened his ears.

Levi thrust the hot poker at the snarling creature's face again and again, but that didn't stop him. The cat crouched low and leapt.

Cat screams mingled with Franzi's cries and Levi's own harsh yells for several seconds. After what seemed to Levi like hours, the beast gave one last garbled roar, turned tail and bounded off into the rocks bordering the stream.

Levi tossed the branch back into the fire and fell to his knees beside Franzi. Feathers from her shredded sleeping bag floated on the smoky air.

Levi's stomach twisted.

Some of them were tainted pink with blood.

CHAPTER FIVE

FRANZI CLUTCHED the torn sleeve of her shirt and struggled to free the material from the zipper. She seemed oblivious to the blood oozing between her fingers.

Levi brushed her hands aside. "Hold still," he ordered impatiently, unaware that his own fingers weren't quite steady.

"Go check our mules, Hunter," she said through clenched teeth. "Tethered, they haven't got any defense against a cat."

Her show of toughness annoyed him. Ignoring her command, Levi pulled a clean, white handkerchief from his pocket. With care, he separated the remnants of her sleeve and moved her, bag and all, closer to the fire's glow. A clear look at the three deep gashes turned his stomach. He shut his eyes and swallowed his distress.

Franzi noticed. "Squeamish, Marshal?" Her attempt to joke fell flat. "You'll find a first-aid kit in my saddlebag," she said, when he didn't respond to her needling. "If you hand it over, I'll see to this scratch while you get the mules." She made an effort to shield her breasts, using her good hand to close her shirt.

But he hardly seemed to notice. "Scratch?" he railed. "You call this a scratch?" When her actions of modesty finally did register, he wanted to shake her. Why did she feel she had to protect herself from his sight? What kind of man did she take him for? He started to speak, but her glazed eyes and chalk-white face silenced him. "I'll get that kit," he said tightly, "and we'll deal with your injury together. Right here. Right now."

The night air cooled his fury; still, there was something about the way Franzi DeLisle hid her emotions like a man, instead of letting them spill over like a woman, that was an affront to his ingrained sense of chivalry. He wondered what kind of relationship she'd had with those three sheriffs that had left her so obsessed with being stalwart.

On the quick trip back to Franzi's side with the kit, Levi formed an opinion of the DeLisle men. It wasn't flattering. And what did it say about her mother? In the nick of time, he decided to keep his observations to himself. Because, Levi realized, nothing in Franzi DeLisle's past was any of his business—and he'd do well to remember her future wasn't, either. Not yet, anyway... Not with Eilert at large.

She was still blaming herself, muttering about her stupidity in dealing with the scraps, when he knelt beside her and gently shoved her fingers away.

"The only stupid thing you did was follow me here in the first place." His teeth flashed a white grimace in the darkness, just before he used them to pull the cork from her flask of fine Irish whiskey and spit it on the ground.

"What are you doing with my whiskey, Hunter?" she demanded, trying to back away. "I don't drink the stuff straight."

"That's a relief. Now hush up, stuff your free hand in your pocket and keep your mouth closed. This worked in John Wayne movies."

"Are you crazy?" she sputtered, the words ending in a yelp as she tried to escape the stinging fluid. Tears came, unbidden. "Did it ever occur to you to use the antiseptic cream provided in the kit? It's supposed to be pain-free."

"Nope." He poured again and winced at her language. "Cream wouldn't be too sterile with my fingers all over it, now would it? You can thank me later—when this scratch, as you call it, doesn't get infected. Unless a tough lady like you would rather watch her arm fall off."

"Damn you, Hunter," she yelled, "not only is that some expensive antiseptic, but you just love inflicting pain on me, don't you?"

"For two cents, I'd use the soap in this kit to wash out your mouth." He upended the silver flask over her arm, and didn't let up until he'd drained every last drop. Intense gray eyes locked on hers. "Of course I don't enjoy your pain. Don't insinuate that I do."

"You wouldn't be nearly so cocky if I wasn't caught like a mouse in your trap." Giving a sharp tug on her shirt, Franzi slipped from his grasp. With shaking fingers, she tried to button her torn shirt.

He moved her hands aside and fastened the buttons himself.

Beyond the stream, the cat snarled.

Levi's hands stilled. "If you're quite through with your little tantrums, I'll bind your arm and see to the mules."

"You owe me a bottle of whiskey, Hunter. And I don't have tantrums."

"Oh, heavens no. You're the picture of graciousness and good sense, aren't you?" He kicked the empty flask aside and unfurled a length of gauze. Careful to maintain pressure on the wounds, he began to dress her arm, his lips set.

"Hunter, if that cat takes out one of my mules, I'll hold you personally responsible." Her gaze accidentally connected with his, and she saw genuine concern in the smoky depths of his eyes. It hit her how badly she was behaving. "Sorry if I seem ungrateful, Hunter," she mumbled. "The ah . . . the flask belonged to my father."

Without a word, Levi picked up the silver container and took special care tucking it back in her saddlebag. Bending to inspect his handiwork one last time, he paused as the cougar's lament seemed to fade into the distance. "Sounds to me like our cat decided to run." Pleased, he half smiled and gave her good shoulder a companionable squeeze.

Franzi shifted, fighting an uneasy spiral of alarm at his nearness. "I suppose the habits of predatory animals are all covered in your neat little city-marshal's manual." Somehow scorn helped her keep her distance.

Tossing the scissors and remaining gauze back into the kit, Levi slammed the lid closed. "What it says in my manual, Ms. Tough Britches, is that women belong safe at home. And so help me, tomorrow—if you're even remotely able to sit on one of those cantankerous mules—that's exactly where you're going."

Franzi's jaw tightened. She itched to slap the thoroughly male pomposity right off his face. Did Levi Hunter think for one minute that she didn't know how inept he was at tracking? Retaliating, she shot back without thinking, "Safe at home—like Amanda was?"

His entire body bucked. The eyes he turned her way were bleak.

Franzi felt terrible. "I'm sorry, Hunter. I had no right. That was way out of line. I'm sorry."

He just stood there, turning the first-aid kit over and over in his hands.

In a softer voice, she ventured, "Would you still check the mules?"

Levi saw that she was truly remorseful. He also saw that her pupils were dilated with beginning shock. He hated being harsh, but maybe this was the time to make an impression. "At last we agree on something. Amanda wasn't safe with Eilert on the loose, and neither are you. This isn't some fun little snipe hunt I'm on. I don't have time to waste taking your mangled body back down the mountain. Yes, I'll go check your precious mules, if you think you can stay out of trouble while I'm gone."

Crow left a bitter taste, and his arrogance was bordering on insufferable. Franzi looked at him through lowered lashes. "Is this where I'm supposed to say 'my hero?' "

Levi made an impolite noise and stormed off. He didn't bother with his jacket, nor did he button up his own shirt against the cold.

Franzi edged closer to the fire's warmth, worrying that he might catch a chill—and it would be her fault. Her eyes strayed to his retreating shoulders, then slid to the slight roll of his narrow hips. Arrogant, yes. He was threatening in a way she didn't understand, but that somehow only strengthened her commitment to keeping him alive. "It's going to be a long night," she muttered around a yawn, deciding not to examine those feelings too closely. Fortunately, the way he seemed to feel about her...well, it shouldn't be too difficult to keep her distance. Marshal Hunter didn't care much for women like her.

If she could prevent it, he'd never know that her nerves were as fragile as a burning branch. Part of her wished things were different between them, but the steps she'd have to take to force him to let her stay would likely only make things worse. Which couldn't be helped, she decided, fighting the lassitude of shock.

It was a fight she lost, and that was the way Levi found her on his return. Sleep was healing, he thought, as he placed a new log on the fire. He was pleased she'd fallen asleep, but doubted he would. The seepage of blood staining the upper part of her bandage worried him more than he cared to admit.

He spread his saddle blanket on the ground and leaned back against a log. Levi was certain the cougar had moved on, but he planned to keep the fire burning until dawn. Maybe he'd use the time to devise a plan for catching Eilert. Except that it was difficult to concentrate. All too often his gaze veered to Franzi.

She'd begun to moan and move restlessly.

He wondered if she was reliving the cat's attack. What if her wound was becoming infected? Should he have used the cream as she suggested?

Levi stoked the fire and took a turn around the campsite—just to check. Fortunately all was quiet. With luck, maybe the cat would find its way to Eilert's camp. But that was wishful thinking. Besides, luck hadn't exactly been in his corner lately. And at the moment, he included meeting Franzi DeLisle in his run of bad luck. He sighed. It was proving to be another long night.

An owl hooted. Levi struggled to keep his eyes open. Suddenly Franzi cried out and thrashed wildly in her sleep. He jerked awake. Quickly he moved to her side, where he placed a soothing hand on her shoulder, only to have it roughly thrown off.

Her eyelids fluttered, and she moaned and mumbled unintelligibly.

The hard ground must feel terrible on her arm. Levi knelt, watching her warily. He knew if he moved her and she awakened, he'd be in for the tongue-lashing of his life. Still, unable to stand thinking of her in pain, he decided to risk it. Surely his shoulder would be a softer pillow.

What surprised him when he gathered her into his arms was how light she seemed. She looked younger, softer somehow, in sleep. Or maybe it was the flyaway locks curling against her cheeks. He wondered why she always scraped her hair back into a braid. Had any man ever been privileged to see it down?

Whoa! Thoughts like that could get a man offtrack in a hurry. Levi sat, carefully settling her in the crook of his arm. Come daylight, Franzi DeLisle would trek back to her ranch where she could fuss all she liked over those homely mules, but he had a job to finish.

FRANZI PRIED OPEN one eye. She was greeted by the gray light of dawn. Somewhere on the fringe of wakefulness, she identified the soft call of a mountain quail. Smiling, she let the warmth of her sleeping bag tug her back into a doze. It was always this way on a trail ride, she mused, wrinkling her nose against the frosty air and the tangy leftover scent of a burned-out camp fire.

She'd allow herself one minute. Sixty seconds of this blissful suspended state was all she asked. After that, she promised she'd bite the bullet and crawl out into the frosty morning to prepare a hearty breakfast for her hungry group of trail riders.

She sighed and snuggled closer to a comfortable thud-thud beneath her ear, and trying to rotate one shoulder to relieve a dull ache that seemed to want to awaken her. Franzi shifted again, and suddenly a sharp pain jolted her back into the real world. Her eyes flew wide. She struggled to sit, but the painful arm refused to support her. She fell forward and listened as the measured beat beneath her ear become a wild scramble of sound.

Raising her head a fraction, Franzi screamed. She found herself nose to nose with an unshaven man.

Hunter felt the sting of cold morning air against his naked chest. Even then his mind refused to come fully awake. He'd been dreaming of holidays at home, the smell of warm taffy and snuggling under a patchwork quilt in his childhood feather bed—a bed he seemed to be sharing with a shapely copper-haired lady.

Jolted rudely awake, Levi reared back and stared blankly into the green eyes belonging to the lady in his dream. But hold it. He scrubbed a knuckle over one sleepy eye. Never had he taken a lady to his mother's home—and those green eyes were spitting mad.

Carefully he removed his right hand, which had automatically tightened around her slender waist. Desire cooled quickly when the lady blasted him like a fishwife.

"You have five seconds to unhand me, Hunter, and to tell me what you think you're doing." Franzi slammed her good fist into his chest, but almost fell in the process.

"It's all right." Fully awake now, he untangled their arms and legs. "Remember the cat? You were hurt. We both fell asleep."

"This is *not* all right." Primly, Franzi straightened her shirt. She refused to look at his chest and found it impossible to meet his eyes.

"You had a nightmare," he explained in a quiet, expressionless voice. "I thought you'd feel better leaning on me than lying on hard ground. Guess I was wrong." He tore his gaze from her sleep-flushed face. "Look, nothing happened. What you did—wrapping yourself around me—is only natural. You said yourself that it gets cold up here. I think you're blowing this all out of proportion." He ventured what he hoped was a charming smile. "How's the arm?"

Her eyelids fell, concealing a sudden blaze of anger. He had some nerve saying *she* was wrapped around *him*. "My arm's fine," she said shortly. "No big deal, Hunter. What time is it?" She flopped over on her side and reached for her boots. She cried out as a sharp pain checked her motion.

"Sure, I can see how fine you are." Levi steadied her, although at the moment it was against his better judgment to touch her. "It's past time I should be on Eilert's trail. Why do you have to be so damn stubborn? Here, I'll help you with your boots. Then we'll see if you can manage on your own."

"Your perp is probably hours ahead, Marshal."

"Perp?" A frown settled between his brows as he shoved her boots on, then calmly stood and buttoned his shirt. "Guess living with those three sheriffs you mentioned made it easy for you to pick up the lingo, huh?"

Fighting off the wooziness of pain and the effect of his warm hands on her feet, Franzi had a temporary lapse of memory. What exactly had she told him? Surely not that she'd served as her father's deputy?

"My life's an open book," he said, when she continued to stare at him vacantly, "while you've been less than forthcoming about yours. I've got a minute if you'd like to fill me in."

"My father..." she began. "He...we..." Franzi bit her lip and bent her head to inspect the bloody gauze wrapped around her arm. "We were very close." Normally, she'd always been scrupulously honest. But to tell Hunter the whole truth would only make things more difficult if it came to a showdown between them. Of course, she hadn't counted on acting like a love-starved fool any time he touched her, either. All she had wanted was to keep him safe. It might be contrary to his own desires, but she would do anything necessary to protect this lawman from the consequences of his dangerous pursuit. Shuddering, Franzi avoided Levi's solicitous gaze and massaged her arm below the bandage.

"Hey, I'm sorry," he said. "I didn't mean to remind you of unpleasant things. You've had quite enough, dealing with that cat attack. Let me put some fresh dressing on that arm before I take off."

He bent to retrieve the saddlebag containing the first-aid kit. "I hope you feel well enough to get back to the ranch on your own. I'd hate to lose Popeye now that I'm this close." His gaze left her and skipped to the narrow trail leading uphill, where it disappeared into a thicket of trees.

There it was again, that infuriating single-minded preoccupation with his mission. She couldn't even begin to count how many times she'd been shut out by that same look, that same obsession. But at least this made it easier to do what she needed to do.

Franzi worked to keep her features neutral. "You know, Hunter, my arm really hurts." *That* wasn't a lie, anyway.

"Is it swollen?" Levi asked, suddenly concerned. "Let me see."

She pulled away. "I'm afraid these scratches will start bleeding again if you remove the bandage." She tried to inject just the right touch of anguish. "Tell you what," she said, pulling out of his hold. "My friend, Kendra Peters, is a nurse practitioner. Her husband, Jared, is the park ranger just over the ridge at station five." She pointed up the trail he was intending to travel. "Kendra will have proper medical supplies."

He wanted to refuse. Everything in him screamed that he should.

Franzi crossed her fingers behind her back. "It's actually closer to Kendra's," she lied, "than it is to to the ranch." Funny how falsehoods just seemed to roll from her tongue where Hunter was concerned. She promised herself that this was positively the last one.

Levi closed his eyes and massaged his brow. "Okay. But that's the absolute end of the line for you. From the ranger's station, I go after Eilert alone." He hoped he sounded determined enough; she didn't listen well.

Franzi gave a brisk nod. Then, although she hated doing it, she had to ask if he'd mind saddling JoJo. What made that request palatable was knowing she hadn't made it just to give credence to her story. She really couldn't lift a saddle just now with one arm.

Levi took care of everything. He even fashioned a makeshift sling out of one of his cotton shirts and helped her mount.

"Thanks," she mumbled. Gratitude was hard—especially since the sling smelled of the soap he used and the woodsy scent he wore. They certainly made it difficult to remain immune and to act unaffected. Luckily he didn't appear to notice anything amiss.

They'd been riding for more than an hour when Franzi reined in and pointed out an abandoned campsite. "Your suspect spent last night there, Hunter. I'll check the coals and tell you how much lead he has today."

"He's not a suspect—he's guilty as sin," Levi reminded her. "It's enough to know I'm still on his trail. I guarantee he won't escape this time."

Franzi shivered. She kicked her feet free of the stirrups and dismounted with less than her usual grace. "You aren't planning on doing anything foolish, are you, Hunter? I mean, you do intend to take Eilert back for trial?"

"As opposed to what?" he asked, glaring down at her.

"Don't get huffy." She shrugged. "I've heard stories about lawmen who take sentencing into their own hands."

"Take my word for it, I'm not one of them." He couldn't help wondering if any of the DeLisles were. Perhaps that was why she wouldn't discuss them.

Franzi had suspected Levi had scruples like her father's, but now she knew he was touchy about them, as well. Touchy enough to make her hide a smile. "Eilert slept late, too, I'd say. And Cricket's really favoring her hind leg this morning." She turned thoughtful eyes his way. "I hope Eilert sticks to the trail and doesn't try to change mounts at the ranger station. Kendra's husband may look impressive in a uniform, but he's no gunslinger."

When Levi gave her a questioning glance, Franzi shrugged. "This is a small community. We were all best friends in school."

"Let's get a move on." His voice was curt, and he boosted her into the saddle with too much force. Franzi hadn't seen how cold-bloodedly Popeye had shot Mandy and left her to die. He couldn't forget, and it was enough to make him urge Rebel to move faster. Nor did he slacken his pace when Franzi started to lag, stopping at more frequent intervals to adjust her sling. He felt guilty when he saw that her cheeks had lost color and gleamed palely in the filtered sunlight.

But he reasoned that the sooner they reached their destination, the quicker she could get treatment—and the sooner he could get his hands on Eilert. He kept a close watch on her out of the corner of his eye. She was so darned stoic. She reminded Levi of a photograph on his mother's mantel. A late-nineteenth-century pioneer woman with a most determined look on her face. It struck him that a man would be fortunate to have such a woman by his side.

He glanced at her ramrod back and worried that he was pushing too hard. Thank goodness he hadn't left her to ride out alone. He'd never have forgiven himself if she'd collapsed along the way.

Just when he believed he might have to let her pause for a break, whether she asked for one or not, they arrived at their destination. A sturdy log cabin stood nestled within a grove of massive pines. A huge German shepherd, with a mouthful of sharp teeth and a ferocious snarl, took his duty of guarding the cabin seriously. "Good dog," murmured Levi, hoping that if Eilert had come this way, the dog's seriousness might have deterred him.

He leaned from the saddle and extended his hand toward the dog. Rebel wasn't nearly so fearless. He flattened his ears, brayed loudly and backed away from the split-rail fence, slamming into Franzi's mount.

Although pain radiated up her arm, she soothed her mule and Levi's, too. Then she quieted the big dog. "Under all that bluster this mutt's a pussycat," she said, catching Levi's eye.

"Sure." On discovering she had fresh blood on her bandage, he cut the sarcasm. "Hey, let's get you inside." Swinging down, he reached up to assist her.

As Franzi slid down the length of him, every nerve in her body went on red alert. What was there about his touch that seemed to feel like a 220-volt jump start?

If Levi felt the same jolt, he didn't show it. "Is it always this quiet around here?" He cast a glance into the trees, totally missing how she trembled in his arms.

"I haven't been here since last summer." Taking a deep breath, she got control of her wayward senses. "It's early for campers, but Jared has a big territory. Sometimes Kendra rides with him. Why?"

"Where'd you last see Eilert's tracks?"

She wrinkled her nose. "Ground's been too hard for the last couple of miles to get a fix. Nothing but shale along here. But any man, even one as desperate as Eilert, would be a fool to stray very far off the marked trail, unless he specifically knew the ranger station was here. The direction he was headed, he'd have to be part goat to attempt scaling that ridge to come in the back way."

"Wouldn't bother me any to take him out of here in a stretcher. But that's the trouble with bad guys," Levi ground out. "They have nine lives to a lawman's one."

He missed the chill look on Franzi's face.

Gripping her elbow, he propelled her toward the house. "Shall we see if anyone's home? If not, I don't know what I'm going to do with you."

"Me?" Franzi pulled free and dashed ahead to beat him to the porch. "I'll take care of myself, Hunter. I always have." Then she tripped going up the steps and was forced to make a grab for the porch railing.

"Sure you will," he shot back, reaching around her to hammer loudly on the door. "Why don't you quit acting so tough and admit you're about played out?"

"In a pig's eye, Marshal. If you think I'm going to quit before I get Cricket back, you're sadly mistaken."

"Now, just a minute..." Levi tucked his thumbs under his belt and was just warming up for battle, when the door was flung open by a petite harried-looking brunette.

"Oh, thank goodness you're here!" the woman said. "I hope you brought more climbing gear. Jared just radioed that it looks like at least one of those two hikers will have to be roped down the face of Old Baldy. Come on in and help yourselves to hot coffee while I plot you two a map."

"Kendra?" Franzi stepped in front of Levi and opened the screen.

"Franzi?" The brunette whirled. Her surprise was instantly replaced by a welcoming grin. "The Mountain Rescue unit didn't tell me who was coming. Oh, my Lord, Franzi! What happened?"

"I'm not here for a rescue, Kendra. This is Federal Marshal Levi Hunter. He's tracking a felon out of Utah. Has Jared got some injured climbers?"

"First, you need medical attention," Levi said firmly, stepping forward.

Franzi shrugged away his hand.

If their hostess noticed his proprietary manner, she didn't let on. Instead, she ushered them into a large airy kitchen and offered them seats at a round oak table. A battered radio unit with glowing green dials took up most of the space between the refrigerator and the back door of the cabin.

No sooner were they seated with mugs of coffee in front of them than heavy static filled the room. Kendra paused, both arms loaded with medical supplies. She cocked an ear to hear the man's voice crackling over the system. A relieved sigh escaped her lips when Jared announced that he'd reached the first climber. However, his next declaration caused frowns around the table.

"Reaching the second kid might not be quite so easy, Kendra. I think he's immobile, too. Any word on the ETA of that team?" His voice sounded strained.

"Tell Jared it doesn't matter when the team arrives. We'll come give him a hand with his rescue just as soon as you truss me up." Franzi gripped her friend's arm.

"Now wait a minute," Levi broke in. "I'm following an escaped criminal, and you aren't in any shape to rescue a flea, much less a man."

"Two men, it sounds like," Franzi pointed out. "And Jared's alone. Maybe the city women you know would leave a friend in the lurch, Hunter, but out here in the country, we wouldn't consider it."

"Meaning city cops have no heart? Are you by any chance looking for a repeat of last night? If so, lady, just keep pushing me." Levi brought up the kiss for no other reason than the hope that it would make her back off.

Franzi suffered blotches of heat. She would have had plenty to say to him if she hadn't seen Kendra's face. Kendra was an incurable romantic, and this definitely piqued her interest. Franzi settled for a dirty look thrown Hunter's way.

The nurse relayed information of Franzi's arrival to her husband, then described her injury. She promised to call him back the moment the team arrived. "So," she said briskly, rounding the table, "let's take a look at that arm, Franzi. How long since you had a tetanus shot?"

Levi wrapped his fingers around his coffee mug and snorted. "A lady who chews nails and spits out barbed wire like this one probably needs a double dose."

The nurse grinned, but her smile faded as she peeled away the old gauze and bared the wound. "Ouch, Franzi. Looks almost as bad as when you were grazed by that bullet."

"Bullet?" Levi straightened in his chair. "What happened?"

Franzi didn't answer.

Kendra had no such compunction. "Cattle thieves, Marshal. They pinned her dad in a box canyon. Wade sent her out of the valley for help. A stray shot nicked her. She refused medical attention and led other deputies back in. It was my first emergency-room duty. I'll never forget how much blood she lost." Kendra's voice caught and she had to swallow hard. "We almost lost two DeLisles that day."

Franzi closed her eyes.

"Oh, Franzi," Kendra sounded genuinely distressed. "I'm sorry. It's much too soon after Gage. Jared and I hated missing his funeral." She swabbed Franzi's arm and dusted on antibiotic powder.

"That's all right, Kendra," Franzi murmured. "I got your message about rescuing that pilot from the downed chopper."

Levi had a hundred questions.

Kendra must have noticed, because she started filling him in. "I wonder if you know all the DeLisles have served as Alano County Sheriff, Marshal?"

Before her chatty friend ruined all her plans, Franzi caught Kendra's eye and gave a warning shake of her head.

Although puzzled, Kendra ended her story rather abruptly. "In the face of all that's happened, it's a surprise Franzi consented to be your guide."

Now she'd done it. Franzi rolled her eyes. Unfortunately she found herself meeting Levi's black gaze.

"She isn't my guide. What on earth gave you that impression?"

Kendra stared in confusion from one to the other. "Why, I . . . uh . . . Daryl Parker told Jared."

"Well, that explains it," said Franzi, kicking Kendra's shins under the table. "Daryl called the morning the marshal was heading out. I probably mentioned I was going to point out his suspect's tracks or something."

"Agreeing to that was my first mistake," Levi growled.

Kendra changed the subject altogether, asking if Franzi was allergic to penicillin. Still, Levi's tone made her laugh as she filled a syringe. "Oh, that's rich, Franzi. What kind of tricks have you been pulling on this nice man to make him say such a thing?"

"None. Could we get on with the shot, Kendra?"

Thinking Franzi looked entirely too guilty, Levi leaned back in his chair. "I don't know that you'd call it a trick, but she goes out of her way to make me think she's tough. She's also bent on having the last word."

Kendra winked. "You sound like all the other disgruntled men in Alano County, Marshal. Our Franzi outrides, outshoots, and outtracks every one."

"Is that a fact?" Steely-eyed, Hunter watched Franzi accept the shot of penicillin without flinching.

"I can't tell you how relieved I am to hear I finally have something in common with the men of Alano County," he said. "I've been led to believe I lack certain qualities of theirs. *Manly* qualities."

"Franzi! Shame on you," Kendra scolded. "Here—step around the corner and put on this flannel shirt. Yours has about had it."

"Thanks, Kendra." Franzi delivered her comeback from the other side of the wall. "Hunter suffers from old-fashioned chivalry, and I believe he took that piece of conversation out of context."

Wearing the clean shirt, she marched back into the room to the sound of Levi's guffaws.

"Your ideas are outdated, Hunter!" she sputtered. "They're the—" She was interrupted by the crackle of the radio and then Jared's voice filled the room.

"I've reached the second climber," he said wearily. "He's in shock and has fractures of both legs and a whole lot more. Kendra, will you tell Franzi I need any help I can get? And fast."

Flipping down her cuffs, Franzi ignored Levi's protest. She snatched up the microphone and in a few terse words had Jared's location pinpointed on the map. "We'll be there in half an hour," she promised, signing off.

"Speak for yourself, Priscilla," Levi said tightly as he picked up his hat. "I'm going after Eilert. This is where we part company."

"Guess again, John Alden." Franzi pasted a smile on her face; she knew her Longfellow, too—and she was no less determined than Levi. "I'm not up to snuff, as you well know, and Jared needs extra hands."

"You shouldn't go at all, Franzi," cautioned Kendra from the background.

Levi paused near the door. "You've slowed me enough already."

"I've slowed you?" Franzi's eyebrows shot up, as did her voice. "Why, you thickheaded baboon. If it wasn't for me, you'd still be wandering the foothills. You couldn't follow tracks if they were taped to your nose!"

She'd hit a nerve and Levi didn't like it. But he'd be hanged if this time he'd let her have the last word. "Well, that's not your problem, is it, Ms. DeLisle?" he said with soft menace. "Bill me for the use of your mule and go on back to your ranch. The rescue team can't be far from here now—let them handle this." Slapping his hat against his leg, he thanked Kendra for her hospitality and turned to leave.

"I'll go alone." Franzi's frigid tone gave him pause.

"You shouldn't go, Franzi," Kendra repeated, touching her arm. "You're not in any condition."

Levi glanced over his shoulder. It was a mistake. Her cheeks were devoid of color; in contrast, her eyes glittered brightly and he could hear the determination in her voice. "All right," he said, after a moment's silence. "I'll go help the ranger with his rescue. You stay here."

"You don't know where Jared is, and I do. If I go—it'll save time."

"That's true." He turned his hat in his hand. "I don't like it," he said reluctantly, "but I'll agree on one condition."

"And that is?" Franzi lifted a brow.

"The minute those hikers are secured, I'm on my way. Alone. And you're heading back to your ranch. This time, I want your promise."

"Sure," she agreed smoothly. "It's a deal, Hunter." Then she bit her lip. In his rush to get outside, Hunter had failed once again to notice the fingers she held crossed behind her back.

CHAPTER SIX

KENDRA CAUGHT Franzi's good arm before she could follow Levi out. "Let him go alone, Franzi. What kind of help would you be with that arm? Stay here," she pleaded. "Tell me about your Marshal Hunter. He cares about you, you know."

Franzi dissolved into laughter. "Kendra, you always were starry-eyed. I assure you that lawmen like Hunter don't care about anyone or anything—except concluding their current mission so they can get on to the next."

She felt a bit unfair for saying that. After all, Hunter had brought her to Kendra's without quibbling. And except for their disagreement over whether or not Irish whiskey made an appropriate antiseptic, she couldn't fault the care he'd given her, either.

Kendra seemed to see her hesitation and pressed. "Are you sure he's as insensitive as all that?"

Franzi bit her lip. When she'd first awakened in his arms, she'd felt warm. Safe. Protected. Come to think of it, *she'd* been the one to make all the fuss. He hadn't even berated her about not burying the scraps. She could well imagine the reaction if that had been Gage or her father. She would have been left behind on her own.

"You should see him trying to read tracks, Kendra." Franzi picked up her hat and clapped it firmly on her head. Although she didn't understand these intense yet changeable feelings that seemed to plague her at the oddest moments, neither did she want to stay and explore them with Kendra now.

"I've got to go, Kendra. I have to show Hunter the way. And from the sound of it, Jared could use an extra hand—even if it's only one." She gestured to her injured arm. "Will you radio that we're heading up there?"

Her friend didn't look too happy about Franzi's decision, but she gave her a quick hug, then stepped aside. "Be careful," she cautioned. "I'll send the team on the minute they arrive."

Levi didn't speak when Franzi came out. Nor did he offer to help her mount. With lips pressed tight, he let her take the lead—which she did, gladly.

The one time she looked back, he seemed unapproachable. Not that his opinion of her had ever been too high, but now she'd probably reached a new low. What would he think once he learned she had no intention of meekly riding back to Shadow Mountain?

They'd traveled in silence for twenty minutes or so, when they suddenly came upon a fallen tree blocking the path.

Franzi reined in and Levi rode up beside her. "Hand me your rifle," he murmured. "This may be a trap."

"No trap. See? Jared's tagged it for removal." Franzi pointed to a red cloth. "It's been uprooted. Probably that windstorm a few weeks back."

"So how do we get around it?" Levi eyed the impenetrable underbrush on both sides.

"Over," said Franzi, smacking his mule sharply on the rump with the flat of her hand.

Rebel leapt straight up and over the obstacle. Franzi heard him land on the other side.

Franzi laughed at Levi's surprised yelp and called out for him to move farther up the trail. Next, she sent her pack animal jumping over the tree, and after waiting a few seconds, did the same with JoJo.

"If that don't beat all," Levi exclaimed the moment JoJo hit with all four feet on the ground. "No run at it, or anything. I felt like I'd gone airborne."

Franzi looked back at the tree. "I guess I forgot to tell you that's a peculiarity of mules. I'm impressed, Hunter. Sometimes the riders on my trail rides get dumped."

His brows shot up. "Disappointed?"

Franzi grinned. "Hunter, you wound me. I forgot you don't know mules, that's all."

"Yeah," he said. "Well, what other quirks do these rascals have that I should know about?"

She cocked her head to one side. "Can't think of any right off. But you've got to trust them more. They're a lot smarter than you'd think."

"Uh-huh." He swept the Stetson from his head and reset it as Franzi scanned the ground for tracks and moved ahead again.

The trail made a bend and angled sharply upward. Her mind galloped ahead, to Jared and the injured hikers as the mules covered another mile or so. The air had begun to grow colder.

All around, patches of snow clung to granite boulders and pine needles were coated with frost.

JoJo slowed, stepping carefully to avoid ice on the trail. Franzi tugged on his reins to stop him altogether, and she shifted in the saddle to pull her down-filled vest from her pack.

"Wow! This came on fast. I can hardly believe the almost balmy weather we left behind." Hunter zipped his jacket and turned the collar up around his ears. Catching Franzi's eye, he winked. "I have a buddy who'd say it's colder than a well digger's . . . knees."

"You have righteous buddies, Marshal. That's not precisely the way I've heard the ending." Her eyes twinkled. Then she laughed outright. "Do any of your friends or family let go with a vice or two?" She watched him blow on his ungloved hands a moment before she hauled a spare pair out of her pack and tossed them to him.

"Speaking of vices," she said dryly. "Kendra sent a thermos of fresh coffee. Would you like some?"

Levi considered accepting to warm up, but because he didn't want to waste time, shook his head. "No, but thanks for the gloves." As he drew them on, he said casually, "I can't help noticing you drink a lot of coffee, and so does Lisa. I read in a health magazine that excessive caffeine may not be too good for a pregnant woman or her baby." He paused. "You might want to mention it to Lisa—and look into it yourself before you start a family."

Franzi was jolted by a sudden, unexpected vision of herself holding an infant. But very likely the only infant she'd be holding would be Lisa's. Then dark thoughts intruded and made her brusque. "I doubt caffeine's any worse on a mother than being left to raise her baby alone."

"I'm not sure the two are related." Levi patted his mule's neck and urged him forward.

"Lisa is pregnant with Gage's baby. I rather imagine she'll need caffeine to get her through all the nights she has to walk the floor—alone."

"So Lisa's your sister-in-law? She's a widow, then. Hey, that's rough on her. I'm sorry. But you almost sound as if you think your brother got himself killed on purpose."

She didn't bother telling him that it was questionable whether Gage had actually married Lisa. Instead, she said, "Don't you think the possibility was there when he accepted the badge? Shouldn't he have been more aware of that?" When Levi didn't respond, she asked abruptly, "Did you ever wonder if the badge was why Amanda might have decided to marry Adam and not you?"

"I think Amanda married Adam out of love. If she'd loved me, the badge wouldn't have mattered."

"Love," Franzi snorted, "is not the answer to everything in life."

He laughed. "Talk to a man in love, and he'll tell you it is."

"I wouldn't know about that," she said tartly. "Anyway, this conversation's gone rather far afield. I was only pointing out that there are worse things in life than coffee."

"Save your breath, Franzi. I'm not going to fight with you about coffee—or about love." He sobered. "How much longer before we get there? I can't afford to let Eilert get too far ahead."

"Right," Franzi said sarcastically. "There's nothing on earth more important than your mission." Massaging her aching arm, she let silence stretch between them again. His turning predictable was just fine with her. She didn't want to think of him in connection with love. And she, for one, liked coffee. If she waited for love to keep her warm, she'd freeze.

Up ahead the trail forked. Franzi selected the less-traveled path, the one that disappeared into swirling mists blowing off the mountain peak. Rounding the first corner, JoJo shied. The almost nonexistent track fell away into a sheer, seemingly bottomless ravine. A stone, dislodged by the mule's hooves, bounced over the edge and disappeared into oblivion. Franzi's stomach lurched. Of his own volition, JoJo backed up, turned and methodically worked his way to higher ground.

"That was too close for comfort. Are you all right?" Levi's anxious call came from immediately behind her.

"I'm fine," she said, and it was true that her stomach had righted itself. "These are the trails I mentioned at the ranch, Hunter. Cut Rebel some slack. A mule will always find solid ground."

"I realize your mules are near perfect," he drawled, "but do you have the faintest idea where you're headed?" He stood in his stirrups and strained to see through the fog.

"Doesn't look to me like anyone's come this way during this century."

"What's the matter? Don't you trust me, Hunter?"

"Mmmpf." He tugged the brim of his Stetson lower.

Franzi chuckled and touched her heels to JoJo's flanks. "That's what I like about you city fellows, Hunter. You're so articulate."

But her comment didn't provoke any reaction from him. Just as well, because she felt guilty about some of her remarks, knowing that she would certainly have questioned him if their situations had been reversed. And the mountain *was* getting treacherous. In fact, Franzi was just beginning to wonder if Jared had given her the right quadrants when she heard a mule bray in the distance.

"Slow down," Levi ordered, edging Rebel around her mount. "Let me go first. I wouldn't want you barging in thinking it was the ranger up ahead and have it turn out to be Eilert."

"That damned chivalry of yours!" Franzi made a face at his broad back. "This time it's misplaced. That's Shadow's bugle. I sold him to Jared last year. Recognizing my animals by sound is a matter of pride with me."

"All the same, I'll go first."

Franzi rolled her eyes. "Suit yourself."

He did just that, leading the way into a hollowed-out spot near a granite cliff. Outside a small tent a few yards away stood a mule with a mottled rump.

Franzi bestowed him a smug grin.

"Spotted rump. Long ears. Looks like your breed all right, but Eilert's cagey. You wait while I check it out," he cautioned, dismounting.

Franzi sighed and slid from JoJo. "Come on, Hunter. Enough is enough. Let's not go overboard with this gentleman stuff. I tell you that's Jared's mule, pure and simple. Have you forgotten Eilert's riding a horse?"

Levi ignored her and walked up to the tent.

Tight on his heels, Franzi heard a moan from inside. She elbowed past him and rushed forward, pulling back the tent flap.

He grabbed her arm. "Wait! You have no idea what you'll find."

She threw him a withering look and pointed to a shivering youth, pale except for a two- or three-day beard covering the lower half of his face. He lay huddled in one corner. His leg was held rigid by a splint and one arm was heavily taped. "There. Does that look like Eilert?" she hissed.

"If it had been, I guarantee by now we'd both be plugged full of holes."

Disturbed by their voices, the man on the pallet opened his eyes. His acknowledgment was nothing more than a momentary flicker of eyelids.

"Hello," Franzi murmured, placing her good hand on his forehead. "Can you tell us where the ranger who's helping you went?"

The man blinked and groaned. "My f-f-friend," he muttered through chattering teeth. "Are you here to help find M-M-Matt?"

"Is that your pal?" Hunter asked.

The injured climber nodded, waving a feeble hand toward the peak. "The ranger's been gone a long time now."

"This kid is freezing," Levi said in a low voice to Franzi. "You stay here and get him warmed up. I'll go see if I can find the ranger."

"Wait a minute, Hunter." She placed her hand on his forearm. "Have you ever done mountain rescue?"

He shook off her hand and glared. "No, but I've scaled hundred-story buildings going after cat burglars. Will that do?" He snatched up discarded carabiners and a muddy rope coiled in one corner.

"Well, don't get so bent out of shape." She tucked her hands in her back pockets and studied him. "Cat burglars. That sounds dangerous. Did you really, Hunter?"

"No, of course not! I said that so you'd quit yammering. Should have known it wouldn't work." He hurled out of the tent.

Whew! Not only was the marshal more capable than she was giving him credit for, but he wasn't always so calm, cool and collected. Her mouth lifted at the corners. She wondered if he ever got *really* riled.

"Is the cowboy g-g-going a-after Matt?" The cloudy blue eyes of the injured youth captured her attention.

"Looks like it," she returned briskly. "Now don't you worry about a thing. I'm going to go outside to my pack animal to get you an extra covering."

He nodded and she left him long enough to grab her down sleeping bag. That should warm him up. She also dug out the thermos of coffee and her last chocolate bar. Staring at her empty flask, she pursed her lips. Her whiskey would have come in handy if *somebody* hadn't deliberately poured it out. He owed her a pint of the best, and she'd see he paid up, too. One day. If he lived that long.

Despite her anger, the thought chilled her. Franzi couldn't resist scanning the upper ridge for one last glimpse of him before she went back inside. But thick whorls of fog blew every which way, covering the trail, obscuring her view.

As she ducked through the flaps, she felt overwhelmingly contrite. The mountain was unforgiving of mistakes. Had she goaded Hunter to take a risk beyond his limit? All her life she had tiptoed around males and their egos. Why couldn't she even carry on a simple conversation with this one without picking a fight? He seemed different from the other men she knew around Jessup. But he was like any other lawman in his obsession with the job. Ah, but then that was the whole reason she was here. His damned job.

"Are you part of the rescue team?" The young man on the pallet asked, breaking into her thoughts.

"I do belong to a rescue unit," she admitted. She plucked at her sling. "As you can see, I'm not in A-1 condition. Hey, don't look so gloomy. There's another team on the way."

She hunkered down beside him. "How about a piece of chocolate? It'll give you a shot of energy."

"I suppose," he mumbled. "I'm worried sick about my buddy. We were on our way down when he slipped on a patch of ice and disappeared. I radioed for help and then tried to find him. Then I fell, too. Busted my arm and twisted my ankle real good. I kept calling out to Matt, but he never answered. It seemed like ages before the ranger came. He carried me in here and trussed me up, but I haven't heard a thing since. Do you think Matt has a chance?"

Franzi patted his arm and looked away. She'd never been good at giving vague assurances; she'd been on the receiving end of too many empty promises herself.

Funny how her father's last promise came back with such clarity. "Franzi-girl," he'd said. "You head for town. Get Gage. I'll be just fine here till you get back." When she'd hesitated, he'd smiled the winsome smile of all the DeLisle men and chucked her under the chin. *It'll be all right*, he'd said. *I promise.*

Later, in the hospital, someone had told her it was apparent from the amount of ammunition he'd had that he'd sent her away for her own safety. His lack of faith in her ability to stand and fight alongside him burdened her to this day. What hurt almost as much was the way everyone but Daryl Parker seemed to believe that if Gage had been the deputy, instead, well, their father might still be alive.

Franzi's eyes filled with tears, not all of them for this young man. She understood his feeling responsible. The hardest thing to live with was not knowing if she could have made a difference.

She smoothed a trembling hand over the down covering and offered him another piece of chocolate. "Let's wait and see what Hunter finds before you get too worked up. Would you like me to go see if I can help the men or would you rather I stayed to keep you company?"

He glanced up, considering the choice with somber eyes. "Waiting's always worse when you're alone."

"I'll stay." Franzi poured coffee into the thermos cup and lifted it to his lips. Lisa had said the same thing about Billy Lee's frequent visits to the ranch—he brought her comfort and consolation. And Franzi herself found solace in spending long hours working with her mules.

"Matt's mother is going to kill me," the young hiker lamented. "She wasn't keen on him coming. If anything happens to him . . . I mean, he's like my brother." His voice trailed off.

Franzi nodded absently. Levi had made a similar statement about his relationship with Amanda's husband. She'd thought before that he seemed like a man burdened by guilt. If he lost Eilert, he'd feel even worse.

It crossed her mind that she should step aside gracefully when he returned. But then she remembered his by-the-book tracking, and her heart constricted. She knew she couldn't let him go on alone.

Making small talk with the boy kept her from thinking. He told her his name was Ken. He said that he and Matt were freshmen at UCLA and were on spring break. Ken claimed to be the more experienced mountaineer of the two, yet he admitted having no previous experience in the Sierras—which was not only silly but dangerous, in her opinion.

She made a mental note to have a talk with the owners of the sports shop in Jessup that had rented the boys their gear. Apparently the shop attendant hadn't suggested a guide, which was more or less automatic in the business. At least the boys had had sense enough to stop at the ranger station before heading up. Lucky for them that Jared had insisted they take a battery-operated radio along.

They fell silent after that. Strangers could only find so much to say to one another. Ken drifted off to sleep, and concern for the rescuers began to overtake Franzi's reflections. She was just getting to her feet, when the mules outside announced visitors.

She was delighted to discover the rescue team approaching quickly from one direction, and Jared and Levi struggling down from above. Together, the two men bore the full weight of the second hiker.

For a time, the newcomers' combined energy focused on the wounded youth. Franzi kept to the background.

"Franzi," Ken called from inside. "How's Matt?"

Even though the other boy seemed to be in bad shape, Franzi felt Ken deserved to see his friend. With some difficulty, she helped him through the flaps and settled him on a flat boulder. Her nurturing instincts took over, and she pulled a cap over his ears and fussed with keeping him warm.

When Matt cried out, Franzi patted Ken's arm. "They're doing their best to help him," she murmured.

As if to prove it, one of the medics moved Jared aside and broke open a Ringer's Lactate, which he promptly administered in an IV.

"That's to minimize shock," Franzi explained to Ken in low tones. What she didn't tell him was that it didn't always work.

For the first time since the group's arrival, Jared noticed Franzi. He tossed her a wave, but didn't stop to talk; he was too busy building a fire. Franzi didn't think she could have carried on a conversation, anyway. Hunter claimed her attention.

He seemed impervious to the icy wind as he knelt beside the makeshift stretcher in his shirtsleeves. He'd wrapped his sheepskin-lined jacket around Matt. Now the wounded youth had a death grip on Levi's larger hand.

Whatever Levi was doing to keep the injured climber calm seemed to be working. Each time the deep rumble of his voice trailed off, she heard the boy moan. Franzi recalled her reaction after the cat attack. She'd found Levi's touch anything but calming. Just watching him now sent her pulse racing. She had no idea why he affected her like this.

When the paramedics closed in again, Levi disengaged the boy's hand and stood. He was headed for the tethered mules, but then he caught sight of Franzi and changed course. She took a few steps toward him, leaving Ken hunched on the boulder.

"Are you all right?" Levi cupped her chin and studied her pale face. "Why aren't you inside keeping warm?"

Franzi tried, but failed to shake off the strange buoyancy caused by the brush of his fingertips. His gaze had dropped to her injured arm by the time she found her voice. "*You* were the one out there battling the elements, Hunter. What could possibly be wrong with me?"

His fingers caught a lock of hair that had blown loose from her braid. "I don't know," he murmured, his gaze locking on her mouth. "I guess I won't rest easy until Eilert's behind bars."

The intimacy of his look, even more than his touch, sent spirals of heat up Franzi's spine. She abruptly became aware that both members of the rescue team, who'd known her since infancy, had paused in their tasks to exhibit an inordinate amount of interest.

"Really, Hunter, you worry too much. I'm fine." It was true except for her suddenly racing heart. She shifted nervously, and the lock of hair escaped his fingers.

He retrieved the coppery tress and carefully looped it behind her ear.

For some reason, she found his earlier autocratic behavior easier to deal with than his tenderness. Fortunately she noticed Ken was beginning to fidget. She saw the worried glance he threw Matt. Happy to divert attention from herself, Franzi nudged Levi. "Ken over there is concerned about his friend. Can you give him any information?"

Levi let his hands drop. Then he removed his hat and resettled it, which as Franzi had noticed before, signaled distress. Because he hadn't shaved, his slight scowl made him look fierce.

"I was just headed over to get another blanket from Jared's mule. The boy's in shock, and the medic thinks he may be bleeding internally. Sorry, Ken. Wish I could give you more. It's just too soon."

The frightened youth reached out for Franzi's hand. He turned a helpless, tear-filled gaze her way. "Is he...? Will he...?" Ken swallowed hard.

Franzi tightened her grip on his hand. In turn, she looked to Levi, knowing she certainly wasn't the right person to give anyone hope.

"It's out of our hands, son," Levi said compassionately. "We've done everything we can. Best thing you can do now is pray for him." He pressed Ken's shoulder and left to get the promised blanket. "Try to have faith."

Franzi's gaze clung to Levi's arrow-straight back and loose-limbed gait. It surprised her that he talked about prayer and faith, until she recalled that his father had been a bishop. Came naturally, she supposed. But it worried her, too. She'd never seen any evidence that faith stopped bullets.

Ken looked up at her then and asked, "Is your friend a preacher?"

Yanking on the tendril of hair Levi had so tenderly placed behind her ear, she said gruffly, "No, he just has an annoying habit of sounding like one. Really he's a U.S. Marshal."

Ken shrugged. "Not so annoying to me. I needed something. I haven't said any prayers since I was a kid, but I'm gonna try."

Franzi simply nodded. If his words helped Ken, all to the good.

About that time Franzi noticed Jared and the rescue team huddled together talking. They looked serious. Had she not been so caught up in watching Levi, she might have anticipated the message Jared came to deliver.

"If we want to get these fellows some medical attention before dark, we've gotta make tracks down off this mountain. Bill thinks there's a new storm brewing."

One of the team members, a Jessup businessman and longtime friend of her father's, paused to add, "You're coming with us, aren't you, Franzi-girl? The marshal said how you tangled with a mountain lion last night. Cat wounds can get nasty, you know."

Franzi set her lips in a tight line. She was about to reply, when Levi strode into their midst.

"Don't even ask her," he commanded authoritatively. "She's going and that's final."

"Is that a fact?" Her chin shot up.

Levi shrugged and moved on toward Rebel.

Franzi followed. She had no intention of letting him leave her behind.

"I'm out of here," he said. "I have some hard riding to do if I'm going to make up time." His jaw jutted out to match hers. "You promised to stay. Not only that, I won't *allow* you to come. I'm going to get Eilert tonight."

"Really?" Hands on hips, she lashed back. "Well, you'd better pay attention, Mr. U.S. Marshal. Because I've got a news flash for you. I'm coming. And I'm not giving you options."

"You don't say?" The eyes he turned her way told her she was courting trouble.

"Not me, Hunter. This." With an unsteady hand, Franzi dug Gage's badge from her jeans pocket and flashed it before his eyes.

Her friends in the rescue team looked up in surprise, but no one spoke as Franzi pinned the star on her vest.

Levi's gaze was icy. "What kind of game are you playing now?"

"No game. As of two days ago, I'm the acting law in Alano County."

A gust of wind swept through the camp fire, carrying sparks aloft. As the ash rained back down on them, Levi stared hard at Franzi's boots. Slowly his eyes traveled up her pants and vest, until they reached the battered star. "Federal law takes precedence. But even if it didn't, this would be the end of the line for you. You don't get it, do you? Eilert wouldn't care that you're a woman. He'd kill you in a minute."

"I'm a qualified law officer, Hunter."

Levi turned his back on her and vaulted into the saddle.

Franzi kicked at a granite rock and swore.

"Franzi?" One of the rescue team unrolled a travois and, at Franzi's nod, attached the poles to her pack mule. The only other sound in camp, save the whistle of the rising wind, was Matt crying out as the men transferred him to the carrier.

"You're welcome to use my pack animal, guys. But that doesn't mean I'm going back with you." She kept one eye on Levi, who had stopped to adjust his saddlebags.

Jared approached, trying to appeal to her more rational side. "Think of your arm, Franzi."

"I can't, Jared." She had no rational side when it came to Hunter. Nor did it matter that her head told her to go with Jared and the team. Her heart directed her otherwise.

Scowling darkly, Levi rode up and spoke to Jared. "You take her back, Peters. What she's doing is crazy."

The ranger held up his hands, palms out. "You have my sympathy, but I work *with* the law in Alano County, not against it." He smiled. "Thanks for all your help. I couldn't have managed the kid alone. Oh, Hunter," he called, leaving Franzi's side. "You forgot your jacket."

"Keep it." Levi waved him off. "I'll be moving fast enough to stay warm." As if in proof, he slapped his reins on Rebel's neck and disappeared in a swirl of fog.

"Damn you, Hunter!" Franzi shrieked. "I can't believe you're so damn stupid!" She bolted across the rocky campsite and struggled, hindered by her bad arm, to ready JoJo.

Jared moved to bar her way. "Level with me, Franzi. Since Wade died, you've had no use for the law. Why now? Hunter seems to know what he's doing."

Franzi's gaze softened for just a moment. "Hunter's not as tough as he looks, Jared. He can't track worth a damn. He needs someone who knows the mountains." In a strangled voice, she added, "He needs *me.*"

"So that's the way of it with you two, huh?" Jared smiled. "No wonder he's so adamant. What kind of man would put his woman in danger?"

"Now you sound like Kendra. Well, you've got it all wrong." She pulled herself into the saddle, even though it caused her pain. "I mean nothing to him. Nothing at all."

Jared caught JoJo's halter. "I don't think so, Franzi." He gave her a knowing smile. "And you chew on this—Hunter can travel faster alone."

"Dead men don't travel at all, Jared. Now let go of JoJo."

"It'll be dark soon. We've got your pack mule. You aren't even carrying a bedroll."

"I don't plan on sleeping. Step aside."

"Franzi, be reasonable." Jared's advice dissipated in a whoosh of wind. But the acting sheriff of Alano County was already too far down the trail to hear.

CHAPTER SEVEN

FRANZI WOULD WILLINGLY admit to being stubborn, but never to being stupid. She stayed well behind the marshal in order to give him plenty of time to cool down.

Trotting along in the frosty air, she thought about the way Levi had eased Ken's fears. He was certainly an enigma. A man with more facets than a diamond. Deep down where it counted, he was tender and good. The DeLisle men had been honest, but rarely tender.

Franzi vowed that when she caught up to him, she'd make a special effort to clean up her act. No more swearing. He seemed to want his women to be ladies. She smiled to herself. Would he even notice? Maybe. Few of her shortcomings escaped him.

Speaking of shortcomings, Franzi thought either it was sheer dumb luck, or Marshal Hunter's tracking skills had improved. From what she was able to discern, he was not only on Eilert's trail, but was closing the gap fast.

A ripple of uneasiness skittered up her spine as she cast a glance toward the darkening sky. With any luck, daylight would hold out and the storm would hold off until she could catch up with Hunter and help him get the job done.

Yes, she'd let him sulk quite long enough, she decided, flicking her heels against JoJo's ribs. He might just as well get used to the idea of her aiding in the capture before they actually met up with Eilert. And there was something else, besides the prospect of a storm, making her edgy. Hunter was heading into a maze of switchbacks, some ending in box canyons. Her father had lost his life in similar terrain. Franzi shivered and buttoned up her vest.

Hunter was riding faster than she'd anticipated. Late-afternoon shadows were causing JoJo to balk and shy at nothing. When at last she caught a glimpse of Rebel's rump rounding a corner up ahead, Franzi was more than relieved. Emotion stole her voice for just a moment. By the time she'd recovered it, he was out of sight.

"Hunter, wait!"

Rebel's powerful rump was clearly in view again when she yelled, but without warning, the trail took a drop. What little light remained was blocked by overhanging pillars of granite.

She thought she heard Hunter shout at her to go back—which of course she had no intention of doing. Concentrating on the trail ahead, she was caught completely unawares when the canyon below her erupted in starbursts of fire.

Short reports, sounding for all the world like Fourth of July fireworks, exploded sporadically along the trail. The noise went on for long seconds before Franzi began to suspect it was her dynamite—the box Eilert had taken from Henry's shed. By then, she was using every ounce of her strength she had trying to keep her normally placid mule under control. Above the din, she thought she heard Levi hollering. Too late, she recognized that they'd waltzed into an ambush.

JoJo finally managed to unseat her. Franzi's last fragmented thought as she catapulted from the saddle was that yet another DeLisle was about to die wearing a badge. And worse, it was going to happen before she'd had a chance to tell Levi Hunter she only wanted to save him from the fate of all the other lawmen she'd loved.

That word *love* rang in her ears as Franzi hit the ground. Like a rabbit, she burrowed under a prickly bush. She was shocked to think how easily she had included Hunter in the group of men she loved.

Certainly she had loved the others; they were family. Her feelings for Hunter were less easily defined. They were confusing. Volatile. Contradictory. Like what she felt now—a desperate fear for his safety, and anger because he'd led them straight into an ambush.

Hugging the ground, afraid to move, Franzi listened to her heart hammering in her ears. Ever louder, the small word love bounced around inside her head. It was a silly thing to contemplate with her face in the dirt and JoJo's breath tickling her cheek. Franzi wriggled experimentally, needing to ease the weight on her injured arm.

She should be thinking about getting back to Lisa—not about going up against a crazed killer. She had nothing but her twenty-two. And that egocentric lawman only carried one, insignificant revolver. She hoped he'd at least gotten around to cleaning it.

Then, as if struck by lightning, Franzi realized there was a very real possibility of Hunter's dying.

Where the hell was he? Damn the man! It was his own carelessness that had led them here. How could she love a man who couldn't be trusted with his own life, let alone hers?

Franzi was of a good mind to climb back on JoJo and leave. Let the marshal get out of this mess with his badge, his old-fashioned chivalry and that cocky smile on his own.

She tensed. Where was he? JoJo knocked her hat askew and clattered off down the trail. She grabbed for his reins but missed. In the wake of his leaving with her rifle, still in its scabbard, she was forced to abandon the safety of the bush. She straightened her hat. Its soft suede was stained and battered, but the hat had been a last gift from her father. He'd worn it the day he died. The memory sent a shiver of dread up her spine.

Where was Hunter? You'd think the man would give her some small sign that he was alive. She fiddled with her hat strings. *Maybe he wasn't... alive*. The possibility triggered another surge of panic. Franzi sent up a rusty prayer, the only honest-to-goodness one she'd managed since watching them bury the first DeLisle lawman.

Nearby, out of the shadows, came the whisper of parting bushes and the stealthy brush of fabric against stone. Joy filled her heart—until she stopped to consider that it might be Eilert sneaking up.

"DeLisle?" Levi's soft call floated out of the inky blackness.

Relief swept over her, only to be replaced by guilt, anger, fear, confusion. She couldn't speak.

"Franzi!"

Her name bounced against the wall behind her and echoed back, the echo sounding frantic. As if in warning, a bullet zinged overhead and slammed into a rocky precipice.

The noise jarred Franzi from her stupor and brought with it another surge of temper. She was fighting mad at Eilert, who was trying to kill her. But strangely, she was still furious with Hunter, too.

"Are you looking to get us killed, Marshal?" she hissed, scrambling on hands and knees toward where she'd heard his voice.

A hand shot out of the underbrush, bringing her up short.

Her squeal shocked them both, and she tumbled into his arms.

Another flash of fire lit the horizon; the bullet hit a nearby boulder.

Franzi winced and buried her head against Levi's chest. Not because Eilert's last attempt had come so close, but because Hunter's fingers had bitten deep into her sore arm.

"Are you all right?" he demanded, shaking her. "Is something wrong?"

Carefully she extracted her arm from his strong fingers. "Your sense of humor beats all, Hunter. In case you haven't noticed, there's a shooter out there trying to turn us into sieves."

"Shh," he cautioned, tightening his hold. "I told you to go with Jared. Now keep your head down." This time, he applied enough pressure to force the issue. "With luck, I've got him boxed in."

"Ouch!" Franzi was unable to stifle a cry of pain.

"I knew it, you've been hit." Levi scooted closer and ran a hand experimentally over her arm.

"Not hit. I plowed a furrow through granite with my hurt arm, that's is all. Don't worry about me."

"Somebody should," he whispered. She didn't bother to reply. They waited until the canyon had grown eerily silent. Franzi sat up. "I'm going to work my way over the ridge and down behind him. I don't want a stray bullet hitting one of my animals."

"You aren't going anywhere, lady." Levi caught her around the waist and hauled her back against his chest. "Plant yourself behind that boulder and keep your head down. I'll work my way behind Popeye and whistle for you when it's over."

"You'll whistle?" Franzi literally saw red. "I'm not a dog to be whistled up, Hunter." She tapped her badge. "I believe you're forgetting who's sheriff."

His eyes gleamed like slivers of silver in the twilight. "No ma'am . . . Sheriff. Let me phrase that differently. The local authority is going to park her rump behind a rock and stay there until I say it's safe."

"Is that city-cop talk, Hunter?" Franzi choked with resentment. "If the visiting law was man enough to consult with a woman sheriff," she said sarcastically, "instead of flying off in a childish snit, we wouldn't be in this mess. Furthermore—"

"Enough!" He clamped a hand over her mouth. His intention was simply to silence her—until he felt her lips quiver, soft and warm against his already damp palm. And he realized that touching her was a mistake.

"Do you have any idea how worried I was about you while I was flattened out there in a puddle of my own sweat?" His angry words ended in a little catch.

"You? Worried about me? Ha!" Her words were muffled by his hand.

Levi wanted to shake her. She had some nerve, all but calling him heartless. But then her lips moved against his palm again and a shaft of heat ripped through his body. He tried reining in his emotions. He'd been in this business long enough to know feelings of any kind were dangerous. Especially now, when he was in an unfamiliar area being targeted for death by a man like Eilert. Plus, danger intensified emotion, and emotion made judgment unreliable. He knew that.

Regaining control, Levi tightened his hold and pulled Franzi's head against his chest.

She mumbled furiously against his shirt and kicked him.

"Ouch! You little brat," he said when she landed a solid boot heel to his shin. Incensed, he'd did what he told himself he couldn't afford to do. He slid both hands to the back of her head and covered her lips in a heated kiss.

Shocked, Franzi struggled and made ineffectual noises in her throat.

Sensing her distress, Levi lightened his touch. He hadn't meant to hurt her. "You shouldn't have followed me," he rebuked her in a husky voice.

She gurgled a series of unkind references to his parentage.

Levi couldn't help himself. He kissed her again. This time softly and with feeling. Was it possible the woman honestly didn't know how quickly—how easily—she might have been lost to him forever? Might yet be if he wasn't extremely careful?

Her limbs now weightless, Franzi tried weakly to push him away—until he kissed her again. After that, her anger fizzled and somehow she found herself desperately kissing him back. Touching him, feeling his breath against her face, abolished the terrifying moments of stark fear when she'd thought he might be dead.

Levi sank to his knees and brought her with him. He drew his face away, grappling for air, more than half expecting to deal with her wrath. He was moderately surprised and enormously pleased when, instead, her fingers curved around his neck and tugged him back. In the soft sweet rush of her surrender, all thought of apprehending Eilert momentarily flew from his mind.

Franzi floated. These were new unfamiliar sensations. Not once did she voice a protest as his superior weight toppled her onto the ground. Her hat fell, unheeded.

Absorbing the jolt with his elbows, Levi lifted his lips and allowed himself a moment to cradle her head. Tenderly he smoothed a loose curl over her ear.

Franzi urged his face back down.

In that brief hesitation, something—a small sound, perhaps—transmitted a warning to Levi. Instinctively he rolled her aside and shoved her behind a boulder.

"Hunter?" she asked breathlessly.

"Shh... not now," he admonished, brushing her kiss-swollen lips with a fingertip. "Listen. Something isn't right."

A loud report directly overhead drowned out his warning. A hail of bullets rattled the bushes near where Franzi's hat had fallen.

She tore herself forcefully out of Levi's arms. Reaching for the old suede hat, she clutched it to her breast.

"Are you nuts?" He dived across her body and flattened both Franzi and her hat.

"Oof. Get off me," she squealed, trying to protect the stiff crown. "Damn you, Hunter, you're ruining my hat."

"Now who's trying to get us killed?"

"Well, not me. Let me up." Franzi poked an elbow in his ribs.

"Cut that out and pay attention!" Levi pinioned her arms and strained to hear if Eilert was closing in on them.

Uphill near the canyon entrance, a mule bugled raucously and hooves clacked against the hard granite. Franzi stopped struggling. "Oh, no! Eilert's getting away. Do something, Hunter." She grabbed his shirt. "He must be using spurs on Rebel!" Uncoiling her fingers, she dashed up the trail. Another volley of shots zinged over her head.

Levi, who was still on the ground, made a huge leap, caught Franzi by the ankles and dragged her back. This time, he held her down by force until the last echo of rifle fire had faded and the thunder of retreating hoofbeats was gone.

"Of all the lamebrained, airheaded city slickers," she raged, spitting out dirt and sand. Snatching up her hat, she stood up and smacked it angrily against her thigh. "While you were busy playing Rangeland Romeo, you let Eilert get away. And you let him steal your mule."

"Me?" Levi straightened. "Excuse me, last time I checked, it took two people for kissing." His eyes blazed quicksilver. "Furthermore, who was too involved to come up for air?"

"You're positively disgusting, Hunter," Franzi said, feeling shame set fire to her ears. "That's twice you've manhandled me. I see why you didn't follow in your father's footsteps. You were probably too involved with the girls out behind the barn."

Levi threw back his head and laughed. "Oh, that's rich. Bishops are human beings, you know. Do you think my parents produced seven children by shaking hands?" He shook his head. "I know you're innocent, but I never took you for a prude. And this argument's insane. I'm hitting Eilert's trail."

"Innocent? Prude?" Franzi stumbled over the accusations.

Levi curbed his anger. Something in her embarrassment told him just how innocent she was. "Don't worry about it," he said, sobering. "This was my fault, and it won't happen again until I have Eilert in irons. We'll discuss it later."

Hearing the second-most devastating kiss of her life dismissed in such a cavalier fashion irritated Franzi. Hunter's latest rejection was even more galling than the first. "I beg to differ with you, Marshal. We will *never* discuss this again. Let's just move it. Not only did Eilert get a jump on you, but Rebel happens to be the strongest of all my mules."

Her composure regained, Franzi turned and placed two fingers between her lips. With a shrill whistle, she summoned her own mule. "What do you think you're doing?" Levi grabbed for her and missed. "Popeye may still be out there... waiting."

"No way," she said, feeling smug because both a thin whinny and a loud bray answered her signal. Her conceit vanished the moment her bedraggled Appaloosa mare staggered up. "Oh, my poor Cricket," she moaned. "Will you look at how Eilert mistreated her?"

In the cloud-filtered moonlight, Levi bent to inspect the open sores on the mare's spotted flanks. "She's been shredded with spurs."

Franzi loosened the girth and freed the horse from her heavy saddle. "She can't bear any weight, that's for sure."

"JoJo balks at carrying double." Franzi chewed on her bottom lip. "Too bad, Hunter, but I guess this leaves you hoofing it."

"You're all heart," he scoffed. "You know, I almost hate to burst your smug bubble, but Eilert didn't steal *my* mule. He stole yours."

"What?" She whirled, mouth open, to refute the absurdity of his charge. Sure enough, there was Rebel happily munching leaves. Humiliation warring with anger, Franzi barely managed to mumble an apology.

Levi tried unsuccessfully to hide a smile. "Checkmate?" He moved into the shadow of a boulder.

Franzi could just imagine his lean handsome face split in that insufferable grin. Not only had he mocked her ineptitude at kissing, but he'd confused her so much she hadn't been able to tell her own animals apart. This was the first time that had ever happened.

Levi watched the play of emotions across her face. "If we're stuck, we're stuck," he announced, suddenly feeling contrite for taunting her. "We'll decide what's to be done in the morning. I know now he's not far ahead."

Franzi crammed her hat back onto her head. "I'll walk Cricket down to the ranger station and borrow Jared's mule. It's no big deal, Hunter. I'll catch up to you by sunup."

"Of all the obstinate females I've come across in my life, you do take the prize. I don't know what kind of men you've dealt with, but the ones I know don't leave women stranded anywhere. Not even ornery ones."

She bristled. "Spare me your gallantry, Hunter. If it weren't for this, we could have caught Eilert tonight."

He shrugged. "You told me he'd be crazy to travel in the dark. Can the great Franzi DeLisle actually track at night?"

"A lot you know," she scoffed, "I do it better by moonlight."

"You don't say?" This time, there was no mistaking his double meaning or his outright amusement.

"Do you suppose you could drop the innuendos long enough to get on with the chase? You know what I meant. As long as the moon shines, I can track. Now, let's go. JoJo won't let riders double up, but Rebel will."

Levi walked over and gathered Rebel's reins. "You're certainly a woman who's fond of giving orders, aren't you?"

Franzi's fingers itched to smack him. "I suggest you forget I'm a woman, Hunter. Start by calling me Sheriff."

Levi studied her, eyebrows raised. Did she really not have the vaguest notion how womanly—how downright sexy—she looked in those hip-hugging threadbare jeans? Probably not.

Removing his hat, he bowed low and swept his hand to indicate she should mount first.

"After you, Marshal." She was still smarting from his earlier comment. "I'll be leading Cricket and checking for signs. If I say turn, do it. Otherwise we may both end our careers at the bottom of a gorge."

"Yes, ma'am—*Sheriff*." He tossed her the reins to the injured mare as he swung into the saddle, then let her struggle up on her own. "Eilert took his pack animal and the stuff you had on JoJo."

"Dammit," she muttered, unconsciously shifting her aching arm. "Doesn't matter. I'm used to roughing it. I don't know about you, Hunter—being from the city and all. Can you survive without your fast-food outlets?"

He dug his heels into Rebel's flanks and sent the mule bolting up the steep incline. "Don't worry about me, Sheriff. Someone packed me trail mix and dried beef. If you ask nicely, I might consider sharing."

Franzi had to grab his waist with her good arm to keep her seat and maintain her hold on the mare. It was infuriating—and oddly exciting—to feel his ribs expand beneath her fingers as he laughed.

She dropped her arm and grabbed his belt loop. "Go to hell, Hunter. I'd rather starve first."

Levi thought it just as well that the climb out of the canyon grew tougher. It forced him to concentrate on any shadowy spaces where Eilert might be lying in wait. Provoking Franzi—as long as they were in a safe place—was one thing; placing her in danger was something else.

His silence suited Franzi. She kept her sharp gaze trained on the unwitting signs left by Eilert. Flattened sagebrush, bent twigs and broken shale guided her decisions. They weren't easy to identify in the wobbling moonlight, yet she found enough to keep on track. She gave directions in low tones, and Levi followed them precisely.

His part of the bargain was only to do as he was told, which left his mind free to wander. He speculated about the responsibility he felt to keep her safe. Funny, but he'd never thought he'd feel this protective of any woman again—not after Mandy. It bothered him to realize that even during the years when he thought Amanda would become his wife, he'd never let himself really go when kissing her. Of course, she'd never cracked his iron will—not like Franzi.

He frowned up at the crescent moon, barely visible through heavy clouds. Maybe it was because he'd been less experienced then, and Amanda had always been somewhat fragile. Perhaps that was his problem; he'd been brought up to think *all* women were fragile. Levi gave a silent snort. Fragile was hardly a word he'd use to describe the good sheriff, who was sitting ramrod stiff behind him. She'd fall in the dirt rather than ask for his help—and yet, deep down, he'd sensed a vulnerability in her that he couldn't quite explain.

Along the narrow trail, the pine forest began to thicken. Rebel picked his way down from a ridge and Levi lost sight of the moon. In spite of the denser trees at the lower range, he detected a new icy bite to the wind. He hunched over the pommel to avoid the chill and wished he'd let Jared retrieve his jacket from the boy, after all.

Franzi noticed his slight shiver, although it was a wonder she did, considering she had to hang on to Cricket, watch for increasingly obscure signs, plus keep herself balanced. It was only because she was so intensely aware of Levi Hunter as a man that she noticed at all. But that awareness was one she didn't really want and couldn't afford. Then she remembered watching him give up his jacket for the injured youth. Franzi ignored her own misgivings and leaned closer to him.

Her sudden warmth against his back shocked Levi out of his misery. However brief, the respite from the cold was welcome. Yet he was afraid to thank her, in case she realized what she was doing and withdrew.

For a mile or so he allowed his fantasies to run wild. What would it be like, he mused, to feel the full length of her in bed? Nice, he imagined, as memory carried him back to the honeysuckle scent of her satin sheets. Every now and then, in a crosswind, he fancied he could catch a whiff. Sheriff DeLisle was a paradox all right. A beautiful, feisty, irritating paradox. And more woman than a sheriff had a right to be.

Just then, Rebel rounded a sharp curve, plunging his riders into pitch blackness. Levi blinked and hauled back on the reins so fast, he nearly unseated Franzi.

"What is it, Hunter?" Her fingers pulled free of his belt loop to curl around his waist. "Is it Eilert? Do you see something?" She pressed harder against him to peer over his shoulder.

Levi felt his heart quicken and his reply was more brusque than it would have been if she hadn't been practically cloven to his back. "*See,* Franzi? I can't see a thing. In case you haven't noticed, somebody turned out the lights."

Feeling his tension, she backed off. But then it occurred to her that he'd called her Franzi—not ma'am and not Sheriff in that condescending way of his. For a moment she relented, until it sank in that his tone couldn't have been more sarcastic. Her response was equally so. "I'm afraid we don't have the luxury of streetlights on every corner, Hunter. Out here, we live by our wits. Give Rebel his head. He'll find a trail."

"I know your mules are wonderful creatures, but they aren't bats. And unless you are, we'll make camp here. Slide down."

"No way! I vote we ride on."

"Sorry, we're not talking democracy. That mare of yours is done in."

Franzi did want to rest Cricket, but she also panicked at the thought of spending another night alone with Hunter. Not because she mistrusted his self-discipline, but because she wasn't so sure of her own.

"A dollar says Eilert doesn't know how capable mules are, either, Hunter. His camp fire will be visible a long way in this darkness. If we continue, we'll catch him and still be back at the ranch for lunch."

"It feels like that storm's going to hit anytime. And don't you understand yet that Eilert's completely unpredictable? Besides, he's got all the advantages at the moment. No, we're packing it in for the night. And that's final."

Levi dismounted and Franzi tumbled over Rebel's rump on her way to the ground. It did nothing for her temper. "This is just great, Hunter. You'll roll out your sleeping bag and set about snoring, while I sit by the fire and try to keep from freezing my tail."

"Wrong," he said, making short work of unsaddling Rebel where he stood. "What you said about us seeing Popeye's fire works both ways. We won't be building a fire."

"What?" Franzi squeaked. "How will I keep warm?"

"Even city cops occasionally rough it, lady. We'll share."

"In a pig's eye." She yanked at his arm and spun him around.

"Franzi," he muttered helplessly, finding her cheek in the darkness with his palm. "I've never met a better tracker than you. But you have to know it's crazy to go on in this."

"Don't sweet-talk me, you . . . you—"

"Look," he interrupted, dropping his hand and hooking Rebel to a nearby tree, "only a fool would underestimate Eilert. You don't know him like I do. You should take a look at his computer readout."

"Compute this, Hunter. I am not, repeat, *not,* sharing a sleeping bag with you."

"Suit yourself." Levi rummaged in his saddlebags, found the salve he remembered seeing in one corner and smoothed it on Cricket's injured sides. After that, he staked the mare near Rebel. Then he tossed out his bedroll between boulders, saying, "My offer as a gentleman only goes so far. I'm not about to beg."

"Gentleman, my...foot," She narrowed her gaze against the darkness. "What was that you rubbed on Cricket?" she demanded.

"Bag Balm. I guarantee it won't hurt her."

"I know what Bag Balm is." She picked up the saddle blanket he'd taken off Rebel, threw it onto the ground and flopped down cross-legged. She couldn't see six inches in front of her nose, but there was no mistaking the plop of Levi's boots as he tugged them off. Nor could she miss the crinkle of plastic wrap and the ensuing crunch as he ate his trail mix.

Franzi's mouth watered. She started to hum a country-and-western tune to distract herself—which worked until her traitorous stomach unleashed a loud growl. Franzi froze. Hunter might not think she was much of a lady, but she was enough of one to be embarrassed by the sound.

The crunching stopped immediately. "Dried beef, nuts, raisins—they do wonders for an empty stomach."

His offer was met with silence. "Okay, okay, I'll beg. Come eat. I'll open the sleeping bag. We can lean against this tree and sit under it. Come on," he urged. "It's going to rain."

Franzi remained steadfast for all of two minutes. Then her stomach growled again. Setting pride aside, she picked up the saddle blanket and crawled over to him, just in time to escape a sudden downpour. Luckily the canopy of thick branches blocked most of the deluge.

He didn't gloat, but simply shoved the plastic bags into her hands and began tugging on his boots again.

She stared out at the curtain of rain. "Hunter?" she mumbled around a mouthful of raisins. "I take back what I said earlier."

"Really?"

"Mmm...yes. I'm not usually such a bear."

"You could've fooled me. In fact, I've probably known more hospitable bears." He unzipped the bag and unfurled it over their heads.

Franzi set the packets of food aside and scooted closer. "But this doesn't mean I want you getting killed in Alano County."

As she chewed a handful of trail mix, she reflected that he was sharing his food and his sleeping bag, and she began to feel petty. "Uh, Hunter...I suppose we might call a truce for the evening."

"Whatever you say." He was all too aware that he'd prefer to be sharing the sleeping bag with her the way she had instructed the other night—without clothes. A giant raindrop hit his nose and slid off. Levi rued the day he'd become a gentleman.

"This is kind of cozy, isn't it, Hunter?"

Franzi's husky voice heated up the darkness. "Sharing doesn't mean you get to hog the whole thing." He reached around her and tugged a corner free.

Stung by his sharpness, Franzi picked up the trail mix and wriggled far enough away that the sleeping bag dipped between them.

"Now what's wrong?" he demanded, trying to see her in the dark.

"Nothing."

"Oh, so this truce of yours was just another lie?"

Franzi cursed the rain for making things more difficult. "I never meant to lie to you about the badge, or Gage, but when you touch me—" She broke off speaking and shifted nervously.

Levi groaned. For crying out loud, did she expect him to pounce on her here? Well, he wouldn't. Not that he didn't want to. Particularly if she kept moving away. That she felt such a need to avoid him made him angry. Yet all he could do was shut his eyes and try to sleep. But for him sleep was elusive, even as the hours passed and the rain slackened.

Franzi had dropped off, breathing so quietly he envied her. Unless she was pretending, too. This time, though, her head hadn't found its way to his shoulder. He decided it couldn't hurt to ask if she was awake. "Are you asleep?" he whispered.

She shot bolt upright. "What's wrong? Is it Eilert?"

"Nothing like that. It's not long now till dawn. I just thought if neither of us could sleep, we might talk."

"Oh." She smothered a yawn and turned to face him, shocked to find him so close. Her voice was tight with suspicion. "What about?"

He shrugged. "There's something that has me puzzled. If you're telling the truth about being acting sheriff, why did you start out so hostile? Why did you act like you hated the whole profession?"

She took so long answering he'd about decided she wouldn't.

"I did it for you, Hunter. I put on the badge for you."

"For me?" A cold gust of wind stole his breath long enough for the surprise to pass. "How do you figure that?" he said gruffly.

"You're like my uncle Mark, and my dad and Gage. Not one of them had a lick of sense, either."

"Thanks a heap."

"You asked."

"Look. I've never tried to minimize the dangers of my job, but neither do I take unnecessary chances. And I didn't need your help. Or whatever you call it."

"Oh, I understand. Perfectly. Lawmen think their damn badge makes them immortal. Well, I've got a flash for you,

Hunter." Her tone carried pain, and something else he couldn't identify. "It makes them dead. And dead gets you one line in the local newspaper. Then, a year down the road, a guy like Eilert's out on parole."

"And so you've appointed yourself my guardian angel?" His lips thinned. "Well, considering the DeLisle record, don't do me any favors."

Franzi felt her face drain. He couldn't possibly have hit closer to home if she'd told him the whole truth.

His hands cupped her chin and he forced her to look at him. "Franzi, I'm sorry. Forgive me. I didn't mean to hurt you."

It was growing light. Now that the rain had passed, a halo of dusky gold highlighted the remorse darkening his eyes.

Unable to bare her soul to the man she found so disconcerting, Franzi shook off his hands. "Let Eilert go," she pleaded. "Put out an APB. Let some other fool collect that one-liner."

His jaw tightened. "I'm bringing Eilert in for Adam and Mandy, and you're going to stay out of my way."

Franzi leapt up and covered her ears. She ran blindly down the wet trail, wanting only to get away from Levi Hunter, from what he made her feel. Standing at the brink of the trailhead, she shouted back, "I'll ride with you as long as you're in my county, Marshal. Or else I'll report your unprofessional conduct. Think about the blight *that* would leave on your sterling record while I go check for Eilert's tracks."

He should be angry. Instead, he wanted to take her in his arms and demand she call him Levi, not Marshal in that hateful tone. And here he was mooning, while she was out there doing his job.

Still, they both needed a moment's privacy. He stood and folded the damp sleeping bag, already regretting his thoughtless words. Any woman who'd lost most of her family to his profession had reason for hating it.

Maybe he should tell her that he intended not only to live to a healthy old age but to raise horses in his retirement. However, if he acknowledged her fears to even that extent, she probably wouldn't allow him any authority. She refused to realize that Paul Eilert wasn't your run-of-the-mill criminal. Besides, someone needed to teach her that she couldn't always have the last word, and that a person couldn't always set conditions on love.

Love? Levi shook his head. He felt responsible, yes. Protective, maybe. But love? He put away the jar of cream he'd been using on Cricket and stared at his trembling hands. Phew! Thank goodness she wasn't here to see.

Come to think of it, where *was* she?

As if his thought had summoned her call, she yelled from somewhere along the trail. "Hunter! Come quick!"

The fear in her voice sent dread through his heart. Had she encountered another cougar? Fallen? Met up with Eilert? Any one of those possibilities made his blood run cold. He set off at a dead run and arrived panting, only to find her kneeling at a fork in the trail. All he could see was a patch of mud. "What is it now?" he snapped.

She looked up, worry etched between her brows.

Instantly he dropped beside her. "Tell me." He gently touched her hand.

"Eilert's changed direction," she whispered. "But I can't tell exactly when he was here. The tracks are sort of confused in this mud."

"So where's he headed now? L.A.? He has friends in L.A."

"I wish," she said, gripping his fingers. "Unfortunately this trail goes back down—and it leads straight to my ranch."

Their eyes met. For a moment, each weighed what that meant.

CHAPTER EIGHT

LEVI GRABBED Franzi's elbow and jerked her to her feet. "You're only guessing, right? I mean, we're sitting on top of a blasted mountain. You can't know Eilert's headed for your ranch."

Franzi blinked. She knew what happened when a man like Hunter saw his control crack—when his mission looked as though it was slipping through his hands.

"My ranch is where this trail ends," she pointed out. "JoJo has made this loop so many times on our pack trips once he's on his way to the barn, it takes a lot to dissuade him. Eilert could have bullied my horse, but a smart mule is thinking all the time about how to get what he wants."

"Rather like his trainer, you mean? Stubborn."

"This isn't funny."

"You're right. Eilert is no joke. Let's mount up and follow him. We should know before long if he changes course again. I assume there *are* more forks in this trail?"

Franzi looked grave. "The trail goes from here to Convict Lake, follows the outline of the lake along the eastern edge, then it takes a sharp swing west. From there, it goes downhill until it splits at the north border of my pasture. The main trail continues on into Jessup."

"Now you've got to be joking. There's a place called Convict Lake?"

"Yes. Five train robbers once pulled a prison break and holed up there. For months they eluded everyone—even the best Pinkerton agents. So you see, Hunter, you city cops don't always get your man."

Levi refused to argue. Striding back to camp ahead of her, he made short work of saddling Rebel.

"Cricket's sides look better today," Franzi ventured a moment later, as she threw a bridle over the mare's head. "How on earth did you happen to have Bag Balm with you?"

"It was in my saddlebag. I figured you packed it."

Franzi smiled. "That explains it. Henry fixed your pack. He thinks of the animals first. He's a good man." She smoothed a hand down her mare's nose. "I don't know what I'd do without him since Gage..." She gazed off toward the ranch. Worry softened her voice and furrowed her brow.

"Maybe Lisa will keep the DeLisle name going. If her baby's a boy." Levi thought happier conversation might take Franzi's mind off Eilert.

"Lisa said she and Gage went to Mexico to get married. But we can't find the certificate anywhere." Her frown deepened.

"You mean her baby might not be a DeLisle?"

She focused on him again and flushed. "No. I'm sure it is."

"Ah...so Gage wasn't perfect?"

"Show me a lawman who is," Franzi snapped. "They only think they are, more's the pity."

"Let's go." Levi found it frustrating that she continued to blame Gage's profession for his death. Except, of course, that it wasn't just Gage. There were her father and uncle, too. He'd do well to remember that. Still, after swinging into the saddle and offering her a hand up, he couldn't help saying, "I wish you'd quit lumping us all together. We aren't cut from the same cloth."

"Now, there's a thought. And he expresses himself with such originality, too."

Levi gave up then. "How many hours do you think Eilert has on us now?"

Franzi's arm automatically slid around his waist, which was a good thing today, because she was forced to duck as Rebel broke free of the trees. But she didn't like being beholden to him in even such a small way.

"Too much mud for me to get a good fix," she said near his ear. "I told you that already. The tracks all mush together. I'd feel better seeing if he camped last night."

Her breath brushed his neck and Levi felt the fine hairs rise in response to the concerns she *didn't* voice. "You don't mean Eilert rode all night, do you, Franzi?"

"Maybe." Her stomach knotted. She feared Eilert had done just that.

"Maybe? What's that mean? I thought you told me only a fool would travel the Sierras at night."

"I was talking about the high mountain trails."

He gazed into a deep ravine. "You call this the subbasement?"

"You've got to quit thinking in city terms, Hunter. Eilert's tracks lead down. JoJo knows the way. I already explained that. Why are you being so argumentative and crabby about everything today?"

"Oh, I don't know. Maybe it has something to do with sitting awake under a dripping tree all night, watching you snore."

"I do not snore. Do I?"

His response was terse. "No. You slept like a baby."

"So why are you mad?"

"I'm not mad. And what's my disposition got to do with our situation, anyway, lady?"

"Nothing." Her tone frosted. She scooted back and dropped her hand from his waist. "And that's Sheriff to you, Hunter," she reminded him tartly.

"Just once, I'd like to hear you call me Levi." This time he was determined to have the last word.

"Not on your life, Marshal," Franzi said sweetly.

Levi sighed. Let her have it—the last word. He wasn't up to sparring with her all the way to the ranch. Instead, he concentrated on what she'd said about Eilert's maybe riding all night. Adam's grief-stricken face flashed before his weary eyes. All too acutely, Levi was again reminded of the gravity of his mission.

They rode two hours without finding any sign of a recent campsite. After a third grueling hour of traversing rocky terrain, they reached a lower elevation where the patches of snow had disappeared and the trail was less slick. In a short time, they left the safe covering of ponderosa pine and were exposed to an open grassy field on the left. Warily, Levi turned Rebel south to follow a tumbling creek.

Thin rays of sun warmed the air, and every so often, spring wildflowers poked colorful faces up through mossy creek banks and nodded at them in the pleasant breeze. Levi might have enjoyed the scenery if he hadn't been worried about the possibility of Eilert's pulling another ambush. He didn't know which was worse—that, or picturing him at Franzi's ranch. If she lost Lisa and Gage's baby, after the others . . . Levi refused to finish the thought.

"Hunter." The elevation had dropped another thousand feet when Franzi broke the silence. "Cricket's dragging her back leg really badly."

Levi made a sound of frustration.

"I know," she said, surprising both of them by placing a soothing hand on his arm. "I'm upset, too, but it won't help to kill a good brood mare. And I could use a break. Rebel's rump is darned bony."

Levi reined in as she requested and waited impatiently for her to dismount. She wasn't quick about it and he couldn't help but see her vigorously massage her backside. "Now you know how I felt," he teased. "The rumble seat on this thing doesn't quite ride like a rocking chair, does it? I believe that was your description."

"And you delight in reminding me, don't you?" Franzi sneaked her hand into her back pocket for a last discreet rub. "Want to trade places?"

"Not a chance." He couldn't contain a dry chuckle. "It's bad enough that I have to look at this beast's ugly ears for days on end, let alone be skewered by his posterior."

"I knew I should have given you LeRoy."

"Why? Is LeRoy prettier?"

"No. He has a nasty habit of taking a chunk out of your butt if you stand too near his head."

Levi doffed his hat. "And I was just beginning to think you liked me, Sheriff."

She smiled and pulled off her own hat, then set about re-braiding her hair. They'd been riding so fast the shorter strands around her face had shaken loose. She happened to glance up and discovered Levi watching her with a strange intent look. Embarrassed, she took a deep breath. "What, Hunter? You've never seen a woman braid her hair before?"

He cleared his throat and reached out to capture a loose curl. "You ever wear it down?"

Suddenly uncomfortable, she stepped back. "Not often. It gets tangled in things when I'm working. Besides, it's heavy and hot. Why do you ask?"

Levi almost groaned. Her innocent comment conjured ideas he didn't care to discuss under present circumstances. Turning away, he busied himself unearthing their one canteen. "Is that water in the stream good for drinking?" He found it smarter to change the subject.

"A drink sounds heavenly. The water here is better than good. It's clean and icy cold." She relieved him of the container. "I'll fill our canteen if you'll bring the animals."

Anything to distance himself from her just now. Otherwise, how could he hope to protect her from the likes of Eilert? And protect her he would—although he'd never felt a greater need for the kind of self-discipline he'd learned from his father.

Levi went downstream with the animals and knelt to slake his thirst. The cold water helped restore his equilibrium. Enough so that he could at least look at Franzi and manage an ordinary question. "How far are we from the ranch?" he asked, rejoining her on the bank.

She licked water from her lips, unaware that his jaw tightened and his gaze followed the path of her tongue. "If we don't stop again, we should get there by late afternoon."

"That long?" Would he last? With her riding behind him, sometimes touching him?

"Well, you remember how far you rode that first day?"

He nodded. Suddenly, he threw himself at her, knocking her flat against a grassy knoll. The canteen flew from her hand and water rained back, dousing both of them.

"Are you demented, Hunter?" she shouted. "What's gotten into you?" She tensed and followed his eyes, more than half expecting to see Eilert. What she saw was a snake sunning himself on a rock very near where she'd been standing. It was a good-sized rattler. Franzi shuddered and scrambled backward up the incline. "This isn't the first time I've been caught without my gun on this trip, Hunter. Being with you has made me soft."

He quietly picked up the canteen and threw her a withering look. "That snake's not hurting anything."

"No, but he might have bitten me."

"He didn't," Levi said firmly, placing a hand under her arm and escorting her back to level ground. "You should learn to look where you step."

"I don't like snakes."

He picked up the end of her braid and gave a yank. "Live and let live, Sheriff. Come on, you've rested enough. Duty calls."

He led the animals over, and she snatched Cricket's reins out of his hands. "I hate it when you're so righteous, Hunter," she complained as Levi mounted Rebel. She pulled a wry face. "Typical lawman. Always thinking you know best."

Levi tugged on Rebel, but had no luck getting him to move. "Typical mule. Almost as stubborn as his owner," he bit back. His irritation growing by the second, he dug in his heels and pulled harder on the reins.

As if in answer, Franzi crossed her arms, arched one brow and gave a low whistle. She was rewarded by the look of sheer frustration on Levi's face as Rebel trotted up to nuzzle her hand. She sprang into the saddle without aid, then slid as far back on Rebel's rump as possible. "Women and mules are both smarter than men," she said smugly.

Levi gritted his teeth. He let her have the last word again!

Franzi felt his tension, the quiver of his tightly leashed muscles. She didn't say another word, even though she didn't fully understand the undercurrent running between them. She did know when a man had been pushed to his limit—and Levi had. Nothing in the world could have made her touch him now. Except that the ground took a series of sudden drops. Unexpectedly and forcefully, she was thrown against his back—where she stuck, no matter how much she tried scooting back. After a few unsuccessful attempts, during which she almost fell off, and a sharp command from Levi to sit still, Franzi had had quite enough of his male obstinacy.

"Let me down. I'll walk."

"Don't be obtuse. We have one common goal here, and that's to find which way Eilert's headed."

"Right." Franzi's angry breath fanned his neck. Somehow, she didn't think it was his "goal" that made his backbone stiffen each time they accidentally bumped. And despite her very real fear, she knew that goal wasn't what had her heart pounding like a jungle drum.

It was all Levi could do to keep his mind on his job. With her glued to his backside, he was a man tortured. But reminding himself of Eilert's viciousness was as effective as the proverbial cold shower.

Two long hours of hard riding passed before they rounded a bend opening onto a vista of the lake, with level ground beyond. The blessed sight hadn't come a moment too soon for Levi: it meant Franzi would be able to keep her distance on that blasted mule. And it meant they were getting closer to their quarry. Eager to increase their pace, Levi nudged Rebel—who suddenly stopped dead and absolutely refused to take another step.

"What in hell is the matter with this beast now?" he shouted, after nothing he tried—not cajoling, pleading, or threatening—budged the mule. The last thread of Levi's control snapped when the animal turned his head and blinked with an expression of long suffering. "Go, you miserable piece of flotsam!" he roared.

Franzi couldn't suppress the laughter that bubbled up.

"What's so funny?"

"You are, Hunter," she chortled. Gingerly, Franzi used one of his belt loops to help her swing down from the mule's broad rump. "Honestly, you showed more tolerance for that snake. But I've been afraid this would happen, hard as you've been pushing poor Rebel."

"Pushing him hard? You bet I am, Sheriff. It so happens I've got a madman to catch. I knew all along I should have insisted on a horse. Horses don't have these crazy quirks."

"So it's Sheriff now, is it?" Franzi studied him, rather like the mule had.

Levi drove his heels into the mule's ribs again, but the result was the same as before. Nothing. He threw up his hands and dismounted.

"That's one of the big differences between horses and mules," Franzi explained patiently.

"You mean a horse gets a man where he's going and a mule doesn't?"

"I mean, you can run a horse to death, but a mule knows when he's had enough. When a mule needs a rest, he takes it. Like I said before, mules are infinitely smarter than men." Her lips twitched. "Or it could be that you called him crazy and ugly one too many times, Hunter."

"Oh, that's just great. Wonderful." Levi stalked down the trail a few yards, then back. "Fantastic," he snorted again, gesturing at the mule with his thumb. "A killer gets away because *he* needs rest. Do you have any idea how long he intends to take?"

"It's not like they belong to a mule union where they have ten-minute breaks every four hours." Franzi was getting equally steamed. "Of course I don't know how long, you...you..." Then, thinking better of provoking him further, she said in a calmer tone, "It varies."

"According to what?"

"According to when they feel rested. We'll just have to leave him here. You can stay if you like, but that water looks inviting. I'm hiking to the lake with Cricket. Rebel will be along when he's ready."

"Hike?" Levi frowned down at his dusty but still-new boots.

"Come on, Hunter, it can't be more than a quarter mile. I thought you city cops had to pound the pavement all the time."

"I am *not* a cop. Federal agents are used to state-of-the-art surveillance gear. And I should think you'd be half out of your mind with worry over Lisa. What if Eilert's at your ranch?"

She bit her lip and rubbed her sore arm. "I'm terrified," she said quietly, picking up Cricket's reins and starting down the trail. "But I can't force Rebel to go before he wants to." She paused, turning back to Levi. "And I've learned not to borrow trouble. Eilert may bypass my place and go to Jessup to steal a car. You did say he has friends in L.A."

Levi hurried after her and caught her elbow. "I'm sorry. It was unfair of me to take this out on you. It's just . . ." He uncurled his fingers, removed his hat and ran a nervous hand through his hair. "I don't know. This whole thing has me spooked. When I think about what he's capable of doing..." He let the sentence hang. "Is it possible Eilert's mule decided to take a rest, too?" he asked out of desperation.

"It's possible." Franzi shrugged. "JoJo is the one I take on pack trips. Unfortunately I think he's more apt to get it in his head to go straight home."

They'd reached the shore of the lake before Levi let himself be pacified by the sparkling sapphire water. "This area is pretty, but doesn't it make you want a bath?" He looked around. "Thank goodness there aren't any campers here for Eilert to rob, or worse. Does the name Convict Lake scare them off?"

"Not really. It's early in the season. Also, this is part of the wilderness preserve, which means there's limited camping. People mostly come here to fish. Permits are expensive, though, so sportsmen tend to come for a week at a time. Our pack trains won't be starting for another month or so."

"Do you like being a guide?"

Her eyes lit up. "I love it. Out here, it's easy to forget—" she waved a hand "—everything."

Levi found a seat on a fallen log, plucked a long shaft of grass and stuck it in his mouth. "You've had more than your share, haven't you?" he asked softly.

Franzi turned abruptly and combed her fingers through Cricket's mane.

Levi found he wanted to know more about what she was holding inside. When it was obvious she wasn't going to answer, he tried a different tack. "Did the other sheriffs in your family enjoy their work?"

"Did they ever."

He wasn't prepared for the fire spitting from her eyes.

"The DeLisle men ate, slept, talked and breathed their jobs twenty-four hours a day, seven days a week, fifty-two weeks a year. Until they died."

Levi tossed the piece of grass away. "Are you angry because they loved their work or because they didn't like yours?"

Franzi's fingers stilled. "I'm angry because every one of them thought he was invincible. They were all above accepting my help or anyone else's."

He looked surprised. "But I thought Kendra said you got shot trying to help your father?"

Her eyes filled with tears and she blurted out something she'd never told anyone before. "My father had to know he didn't have enough bullets to hold those men off. He sacrificed himself for me."

Levi absorbed what she said and some of what she held back. He stood up, skirted the horse and took her in his arms. Tucking her head under his chin, he stroked one hand down her back. He'd been a fool to think she wasn't fragile. Right now, it would take very little for her to break apart in his arms. Never had he felt so fiercely protective of anyone. Not even Amanda. "A man does what he has to do to protect what he loves. It's obvious your father loved you more than life itself."

She shuddered and the tears began to flow. Her fingers crumpled his shirt beneath the shield he'd pinned on when she hadn't been watching. "But I loved him, too, Hunter. He didn't have the right to decide for me. After all, I was his deputy. Maybe if I'd stayed—"

"Shh." Levi rocked her. "Your father sounds like a true warrior. Warriors shield their women. That's a fact of life."

Franzi swallowed her tears and jerked out of his arms. "That's crap, Hunter. What kind of women do you know, anyway?"

"Nice women." He sounded annoyed. "How would you describe that *manly* man you seem to think I can't hold a candle to?"

"Well, it wouldn't be one of those John Wayne characters you seem to model yourself on."

"Oh?"

"No. Can you see a man like that letting a woman help during a shoot-out? That same archaic chivalry ran through my father, my uncle and Gage. And it runs through you, too, Hunter. No matter how liberal you think you are."

Levi advanced on her. "If I really acted like John Wayne, you wouldn't be on this trip. And you definitely wouldn't always have the last word."

"I don't—always. Quit changing the subject." Her eyes met his in challenge. "Answer me square. Will you accept my help catching Eilert?"

"When mules fly." His gaze shifted to a point over her left shoulder. "And speaking of the cantankerous beasts, Rebel has finally decided his break is over. None too soon, either, I'd say. Shall we go?"

"Gladly. But when we flush out Eilert, don't expect me to step aside and watch you end up a dead hero in my county."

"Humpf." *Let that suffice as the last word*, Levi thought. Jaw set, he swung into the saddle.

Franzi clambered up behind him, seething. If Hunter thought she'd stand by and watch him die like all the others, he obviously didn't know some women could be warriors, too.

Yet, with her decision came a pang of regret. A small part of her, the part buried beneath the veneer of the determined warrior, wished things could be different between herself and Levi Hunter. If only they'd met under other circumstances. If only he understood and appreciated her values—and her mules. *If only he didn't wear a badge.*

Franzi let her anger go with a sigh. One of her father's favorite sayings surfaced in her mind. "If wishes were horses, then beggars would ride." It reminded her of what the marshal said that first night at the ranch—he didn't beg anyone, especially not a woman, for anything.

With a heavy heart, Franzi turned her attention toward Eilert's tracks. The scary thing was that the closer they got to her ranch, the less Eilert had tried to cover them.

Still maintaining a stiff silence, they arrived at the crossroads.

Levi was the first to speak. "I know I'm not much on tracking, but the way I see it, Popeye's leaving an open invitation."

"Looks that way to me, too," Franzi muttered, biting her lip.

"He's not going to Jessup, either, is he?"

"No."

Levi hauled back on the reins. "Any way to get onto your property from the back—preferably without being seen?"

"We'd have to turn here and go west a ways. There isn't a trail. It would take longer, but we could."

"Let's do it."

"You don't think he'll be holed up in the barns, then?" Her voice wasn't steady.

Levi turned and gave her a look that chilled her blood.

The sun was sinking by the time they reached the ranch buildings and slipped into the outermost barn. Franzi led Cricket into a stall and gave her oats, while Levi unsaddled Rebel.

"It's too quiet for this time of day," she whispered. "By now, Henry should be feeding stock. You can hear him for a mile. He sings at the top of his lungs... always off-key." She allowed a tiny smile. "Pirate hates his singing. He howls. Together, they make quite a duo."

"You stay here and keep quiet. I'm going to make a quick check of the other outbuildings."

"I'm coming, too."

"No."

"You plan to hog-tie me, Hunter?"

"DeLisle. Give me a break."

With the sun behind the trees, it had grown cool. Franzi dug her vest out from beneath his sleeping bag. She used her shirtsleeve to polish the dull star still pinned to the left side.

"Back to that are we, Sheriff?" Levi's lip curled.

"Exactly."

"All right. Come on. I don't like it, mind you, but there isn't time to argue. Just promise me you won't do anything foolish."

"I haven't done anything foolish since I lost my father. Not until now."

Something akin to remorse flashed in his eyes. "Catching Eilert is my responsibility. Either you agree to let me call the shots or I *will* hog-tie you. Do I make myself clear?"

"As crystal." This time Franzi's smile didn't reach her eyes. "So long as you remember this is my ranch, Marshal."

"Don't worry, I won't set it on fire to smoke him out... unless I have to." He leveled her a look. "So, if we finally see eye to eye, let's get on with it."

Franzi didn't say she sincerely doubted they'd ever see eye to eye on anything. Provoking him now would serve no purpose. When the time was right, he'd know where she stood.

Together, they searched all the barns and sheds. They had Henry's cabin and the ranch house to go when Franzi asked the question that had been bothering her. "Precisely how do you plan on capturing Eilert with nothing but a thirty-eight?"

He waved her to silence, shielded her with his body and burst through the back door of Henry's cabin. It was quickly evident that no one was there, but he went through the motions of searching every room before he answered. "I said it before—I'm smarter. But I won't pretend I wouldn't like to catch him before he has a chance to arm himself with all those guns in your cabinet."

She felt a need to defend herself. "Ranchers need guns."

"Really?" His look sliced through her defense. "How come all my brothers-in-law ranch and not one of them owns an arsenal like yours?"

"Then it's a good thing Eilert didn't stay in Utah, Marshal." She paused. "Gage kept six rifles and three handguns . . . plus shells for the lot."

He grimaced. "That many? Good old Gage. I was beginning to like him, too—once I found out you weren't his wife." His gaze skimmed over her.

She looked away. He had an annoying habit of getting personal whenever he wanted to shut her up. "Let's try and move a little closer to the house. Maybe he isn't here and this is all a waste of time. He may just have traded JoJo for one of our vehicles."

Levi felt his stomach turn inside out again. "Either way, what happens is my call." Keeping her well behind him, he led them on a circuitous route to the clearing where the cars were parked.

"Hunter, look." Franzi clutched his sleeve and pointed out three shadowy figures hovering near his Bronco. "It looks like Henry and Billy Lee, but I can't tell who the third one is," she said in a hushed tone.

Pirate, who was roped to the door of Henry's vehicle, saw her and started to whine. The men in the circle cocked their guns.

"Billy Lee, it's me, Franzi," she called out. "Will you kindly be careful where you point that thing?" She stepped in front of Levi, then walked toward the group and swept Billy's rifle aside.

Henry squinted through the gathering dusk. "Lordy, are you two welcome."

Levi stepped in front again. "Why is that?" he queried sharply.

Billy looked distressed. "Know that fella you were after, Marshal? He's barred himself up at the house and he's holding Lisa hostage."

Franzi gasped. The third man was another green deputy, younger even than Billy. "So what have you boys done? Is the house surrounded? Are there back-up officers on the way?"

Billy Lee's freckles stood out in his pale face. "Henry's lucky the guy didn't get him, too. Joe and me just got here. I didn't know what to do. The guy's demanding a helicopter and a pilot to fly him to Mexico. If one's not here in twenty-four hours, he's gonna kill Lisa."

"So when's the chopper due?" she cut in.

"I didn't order one," Billy mumbled. "Didn't know how."

Franzi snatched off her hat and slammed it against her hip. "Rick Poston has a small one, but I hate to involve a regular citizen. The army base has larger ones. That's probably our best bet."

"No!" Levi placed a staying hand on Billy's shoulder and glared at Franzi.

She rounded on him. "What do you mean, no? Lisa's just a kid, Hunter, and she's pregnant. You heard Billy Lee say if Eilert got his chopper, he'd let her go."

"He won't." Levi was blunt. "He'll kill her, anyway. That's the way Eilert operates. I'm in charge, and I say there'll be no deal. He can't afford to lose a hostage until he gets what he wants."

Franzi stared at him, unable to meet the unrelenting ice that had edged out the gentleness in his eyes. She reached a hand toward him, then drew back. "You can't mean that, Levi," she said softly, remembering his warmth in caring for her after the cat attack and his compassion for the hikers.

It was the first time she'd called him by his first name. If for no other reason, it nearly killed Levi to refuse her. But when he recalled Amanda, it was all he could do to keep from scooping Franzi up and running until he found her a safe place, miles away from Eilert.

Yet it was precisely because of what happened to Amanda that he had to steel himself against her pleas. "I not only mean it, Sheriff, but if you interfere in any way, I'll see you brought up on charges."

Franzi's head jerked back as though she'd been slapped. But then, what had she expected? After all, he was still a lawman. And this was his mission.

The pain in her heart was so great she didn't think she could abide it. Yet somehow she managed to hide her feelings. If Hunter sent her away, as her father had, he was sure to suffer the same fate.

Lord help her—in spite of her resolve, she'd fallen in love with a lawman.

Love had come quickly; only a few days had passed since his arrival at Shadow Mountain Ranch. But they'd been extraordinary days, of tension, fear... and trust. Now, she knew without a doubt, knew with more certainty than she'd ever known anything before, that she loved Levi Hunter.

And she couldn't bear to take a chance that he might die like the others. The cold hard truth stole her breath away and left her knees quaking.

There simply had to be another way. A way to rescue Lisa—and keep Levi safe.

CHAPTER NINE

LEVI GAVE LITTLE THOUGHT to Franzi's easy acquiescence He simply felt relief. He picked up Billy's bullhorn to let Eilert know he was there. Had he not been so concerned about Popeye's hostage, Levi might have remembered the last time Franzi had appeared to give in willingly—and how it had ended. Instead, hoping Eilert's anger was with him and not the woman inside, he made the initial contact and turned possible solutions over in his mind.

Behind the marshal, within the shadow cast by Henry's truck, Billy Lee frantically beckoned Franzi.

"What is it, Billy?" She resented the fact that he was taking time from her plotting. Surely it didn't take a three-digit IQ to know this was the kind of situation where every minute counted.

Billy rushed his words. "I've done something terrible, Franzi, and if I don't tell someone, I'm gonna bust."

Struck by his sincerity, Franzi placed a consoling hand on his arm. Even in the low light shed by one of the lanterns Henry was distributing around the trucks, Franzi could see the agony in Billy's eyes. "Come on, Billy. You don't have to hide anything from me. I'm worried, too, and Daryl won't blame you, whatever happens. There was no way of knowing Eilert was going to double back. If you'd been the one to go with Hunter, instead of me, nothing would have changed."

Was that really true, she wondered? Would Hunter have captured Eilert if, as he'd said numerous times, she hadn't slowed him down? No, she refused to believe that. He'd needed her tracking skills.

Billy didn't seem to notice her moment of self-doubt. "I don't give a hang about Daryl. If something happens to Lisa before I can tell her... before I can confess..." He shuddered. "I'll never, ever forgive myself, Franzi."

"Confess? Confess what, Billy? Good heavens. Would you quit being so melodramatic? We're running out of time."

Franzi's impatience galvanized him as nothing else had. Unable to meet her eyes, the young deputy mumbled, "I took Lisa's marriage certificate when we were logging in Gage's things at the police station. I knew it was wrong, but I loved her, and I thought...well, I thought that without it, she might need my help."

Stunned, Franzi groped for words. "What... how... I mean..."

Immersed in his misery, Billy didn't look up. "What I'm trying to say, Franzi, is that the way I feel about Lisa is nothing new. I've been crazy about her since we were kids. But I swear to you, if Gage had lived, she never would have been the wiser. Good Lord, Franzi, I've never done another dishonest thing in my life. I hope you believe that." His shoulders bowed.

"But why?" she asked, trying to understand. "What purpose did it serve? Billy, you've let her think—let everyone in town think—that Gage tricked her."

His eyes grew stubbornly remote. "How was I to know you'd take her in? Did you even know her old man knocked her around? He treated his dog better. Gage didn't have time to put her on his insurance, and I was afraid she'd have to go back home."

"After I did take her in, why didn't you tell her then? As much as you've been underfoot lately, you must have known I didn't believe she and Gage had gotten married, either."

She waved a hand. "Gage was sometimes... Well, Gage was... Gage," she finished lamely.

"Exactly, Franzi. That's the whole point I'm trying to make. Gage *liked* Lisa, but he didn't love her. He told me so the day he asked me to cover when they got married. I wanted to hate him, but I couldn't. I mean, she was crazy about him and he did right by her. See, Franzi, when I took the damn license, I thought she'd choose me rather than be slapped around by her pa."

A limp lock of hair fell over his eye. He pushed it back with shaking fingers. "I tell you, the guilt's been killing me for weeks. And now...now Lisa's in there with that monster. I may never get the chance to make things right." He sounded truly miserable.

"Nonsense, Billy." Franzi shook him. "I'm not going to let anything happen to Lisa or her baby. And what about the baby? Are you prepared to accept another man's child?"

He nodded. "That's never been a problem. The only problem's been confessing, and maybe losing her."

"Well, then, you'd better learn how to grovel. I've got an idea. If it works, you'll get your chance."

"But the marshal said—"

She broke in, "He's not God. This is just another mission to Hunter, and Lisa's only another hostage. Listen to me, Billy. I want you to go to Henry's cabin and put in a call to Rick Poston. The chopper he uses to check for stray cattle is closer than the army base. Explain our situation and ask for his best pilot. Tell him I need somebody who can set that thing down a hundred yards from my front porch. Make sure he knows they'll be flying to Mexico—but promise you won't breathe a word of this to Hunter."

"Poston might not listen to me. Shouldn't you go?"

"Billy Lee. You're about to be a husband and father. Don't you think it's time you started acting like a man?"

He frowned. "Maybe that's why Daryl wanted you for sheriff, instead of me."

Taken aback by his response, Franzi paused. Was that how Levi saw her, too? As one of the guys? Without any womanly qualities? She shook off the thought. "Doesn't matter, Billy. I'm going to work my way to the kitchen window and convince Eilert to switch me for Lisa. I suspect one hostage will be much the same as another to him. With luck, I'll find a way to defuse things from inside."

"Hunter ain't gonna like this."

"He can go to hell." Registering Billy's shock, she added in a gentler voice, "You aren't the only one who's feeling guilty. Since Dad . . . well, I need to do this for me. Like everyone else, Levi thinks... Oh, never mind what he thinks. He's wrong."

"Uh-oh. Speak of the devil, he's calling me. I'll see what he wants, then I'll get right on this. I promise you, Franzi, if you get Lisa out I'll throw myself on her mercy. I'll tell Daryl Parker what I did. If need be, they can spread it over the front page of the newspaper." His eyes clouded. "I'll confess, even if Lisa never wants to see me again."

Franzi grabbed his arm. "The best thing you can do for Lisa and the baby is to turn in that badge. Admitting you were wrong is a good start, Billy. But dying in some back alley sure won't help your family."

Levi didn't like being ignored. "This is no time for idle chitchat, folks." He stalked over and thrust a paper into Billy's hand. "I've sent your buddy and Henry around to guard the back of the house. I want you to call this number. Tell my boss I need two of his best people in here ASAP."

Billy shot Franzi a nervous glance.

Levi saw it. "Pretend you work for me tonight, Deputy Lee. Tell the guy at that number we've got Eilert cornered, and he'll do the rest. I want people in here who've been trained in criminal psychology."

"It might be nice if they could shoot straight, too," Franzi muttered.

Levi glared at her. "Thanks to you, Eilert's got enough guns to stand off an army. If he sees us with weapons, it may provoke him."

"Go ahead, Marshal. Blame me if it makes you feel better," she said sweetly. "I can't help it if ranchers have to shoot a varmint now and then."

"Well, there's a varmint holed up in your house all set to shoot ranchers," he snapped. "Now, could your deputy kindly do as I ask, just this once?"

"Do as he says, Billy. Keep your gun out of sight." Franzi nodded. "And while you're calling, don't forget to take care of my request, too."

"Which is?" demanded Levi.

Franzi feigned interest in straightening her vest. She didn't like lying to him again, but sometimes the end justified the means. She sincerely hoped this was one of those times. She avoided his eyes. "You know how long we've been without food. I thought we'd have somebody from town bring sandwiches and coffee."

"No." Levi's lips tightened. "I'm sorry, but I can't give Eilert the chance to take potshots at innocent people."

"So give him what he wants," she challenged.

"There's no dealing with men like Eilert. They have no conscience." His eyes darkened and he watched for some sign of understanding. When he saw none, Levi turned to Billy. "Make that call, while I work out a plan."

Franzi motioned at Billy with her head. "So, Marshal," she drawled, "while we're waiting for this great revelation to strike you, what exactly do you want me to do?"

Levi ground his teeth. He had a nagging suspicion that she was up to something, but he didn't have time to investigate that right now. Giving her the benefit of the doubt, he said quietly, "I want you to find a secure spot and keep down out of sight."

"Sure, but I need a bathroom first."

He rolled his eyes. "Fine. If you want modern conveniences, go with Billy. If not, pick a safe tree. I've got things to do. Our pal Eilert left JoJo and a couple of pack mules roped to your front porch. I'm going to try and turn them loose—in case he decides to start shooting."

"Let me help," she said quickly. "After all, they're my animals."

"I thought I made it clear. I want you out of harm's way." His voice was rough, his eyes haunted.

Gooseflesh rose on Franzi's arms. For a moment, she forgot their disagreement. A strange melting sensation, very like the one she'd experienced when he kissed her, weakened her knees and shook her resolve. "You will be careful, won't you?" she cautioned.

A crooked smile flashed briefly across his face. Unable to stop himself, Levi reached out and ran a finger down her cheek and along her jaw. Gruffly he said, "Nothing's going to happen to me, Franzi. I won't let it. When this is over, we have things to discuss."

What things? Franzi swallowed a lump in her throat. More disturbed than she was willing to let on, she turned and practically ran after Billy. "Hold on, Billy. Hunter's right about the animals. Let's take Pirate to Henry's cabin. He has reason to hate Eilert." For the deputy's ears alone, she added, "I can't afford to have him following me."

"If this guy is as terrible as Hunter says, you shouldn't go to the house."

"Doing something has to be better than doing nothing. Don't you agree?"

"I suppose," he muttered, catching Pirate with a firm hand. "All the same, take my knife. And—" he swallowed hard "—if you do get to see Lisa, will you do me a favor? Tell her I love her." His eyes filled with tears and he looked away.

Franzi took the slim knife and bent to insert it inside her leather boot. For some reason, she found Billy's easy declaration of love disconcerting. The men she knew—men like her uncle, her father, Gage, even Hunter—would never speak so frankly of love. But Franzi had learned early not to expect words or gestures of love from the DeLisle men. Foolishly she'd held her breath and waited after Hunter's last kiss. What he'd done, though, was call her an innocent and a prude. Then he'd declared the kiss wouldn't happen again.

Straightening, Franzi buried the old longing. It was for the best, really, considering his profession. She knew that. Pressing her badge into Billy's hand, she said hoarsely, "Hang on to this." She managed a short laugh. "I won't make any points with Eilert if he sees it." She gave Pirate's ears a quick tug, tossed Billy a cocky thumbs-up and melted into the darkness.

It took her nearly an hour to work her way around to the kitchen window, past Levi's two posted guards. When she slid the window open a couple of inches and heard Lisa sobbing, she knew she was doing the right thing. Surely if Hunter had any inkling of Lisa's state of mind, he'd be willing to give in to Eilert's demands.

Yet even as the thought entered her head, she dismissed it. Of course he wouldn't. Lawmen had ice water in their veins. All they cared about was finishing one mission so they could start another. She'd never known one who put his feelings for a woman before duty. And that included her father and Gage. Why should Levi be different?

Quietly Franzi raised the window higher, then shifted positions enough to see Lisa slumped against the side of the gun cabinet. She looked uncomfortable, her hands tied behind her back with a red kerchief and her face streaked with tears. The glass in the gun cabinet had been smashed, and an assortment of guns, cold metal gleaming, were lined up beneath the dining-room window. Franzi shivered, remembering Levi's concerns.

Eilert wasn't visible, but she could hear him exchanging terse comments with the marshal. He seemed to be near the front door, which gave her the opportunity she needed to speak with Lisa.

"Lisa," Franzi called softly.

The girl roused briefly. "Franzi? Franzi, is that you? Where are—?"

"Shh! I'm at the window. Quit crying and listen carefully. I want you to tell Eilert I'm unarmed. Tell him I want to talk a deal."

"The marshal said he won't deal." Her head drooped again.

"What Hunter doesn't know won't hurt him."

Lisa's voice quavered. "Franzi. This guy is real scary."

"I know. Shh. Just do what I asked." She had no time to duck as Eilert stalked into the room. Franzi's breath stalled. He looked terrifying with his bald head, crooked nose and cruel mouth. And the munition belts banded across his chest...

"Shut up." Eilert kicked Lisa's leg, and she cried out. "Who you talkin' to, anyway?" he demanded.

"Me," Franzi blazed, showing herself. "Leave her alone, you big bully! Can't you see she's going to have a baby?"

"Who the hell are you? Get your hands up where I can see 'em and tell me what you're doin' here."

"I own this ranch. Let Lisa go. Take me, instead." Franzi lifted her hands, showing them to be empty.

"You the dame who's been trackin' me along with Hunter?"

Franzi weighed telling him the truth. "Yes," she admitted hesitantly.

"You got any pull with him?"

"Maybe." She knew that was a lie. "Will you let Lisa go?"

The man shoved a meaty hand through the window and latched on to Franzi's shirtfront. "You're mouthy. I hate mouthy women."

Franzi tried to hide her alarm, but her heart hammered hard in her throat.

"Think you can convince Hunter to get me that chopper?"

With luck, if Billy had reached Rick Poston, it might already be on its way. Franzi decided to try a bluff. "Untie Lisa, let her walk out the kitchen door as I walk in. When she's safe, I'll tell Marshal Hunter to get whatever you want."

He gave a laugh that made Franzi's skin crawl. "A tough lady, huh? Well, you'll be a heap more fun than a dame who bawls all the time." Eilert leered at her. "Hey! You Hunter's woman?"

"No," she said indignantly, wrenching out of his grip. A button flew off her shirt, and when it landed against the floor with a pop, Eilert jumped and pushed a gun in her face. "No funny stuff, you hear?"

Franzi nodded. She clamped her teeth together, afraid he'd hear them chattering and know she was scared witless. Although she wasn't ready to admit she should have listened to Levi, she *did* admit to outright fear. At that moment his words came back—*a man protects what he loves*—and Franzi felt regret mixed with her terror.

"Get over by the kitchen door," Eilert ordered. "Open it up real easy. I want to see you're not carryin' a piece."

"I'm not." But she did as he asked all the same. "Lisa," she instructed in what she hoped was a decisive voice, "stand up and let Mr. Eilert free your hands." Sidling toward the door, she slowly pushed it open.

She could hear Levi calling over the bullhorn, pressing Eilert to show himself at the front entrance again. Franzi wished her stomach could be as empty of emotion as Hunter's voice. Shuddering, she blocked out the familiar deep rumble and bit down hard on her bottom lip.

Once Eilert had determined she wasn't armed, he prodded Lisa to her feet with his gun. Franzi almost fainted from relief when she saw him loosen the younger woman's bonds.

Then something went wrong with her plan. One minute, certain the exchange was a reality, she faced Lisa at the threshold. The next, Eilert moved, quick as a cat, and grabbed her sore arm. She buckled, and he shoved her into Lisa with such force that both women fell to their knees. Before Franzi could even utter a sound of protest, the kitchen door slammed and was locked securely behind her. With real despair, she folded Lisa into her arms and waited for the worst.

UNAWARE OF THE CHANGES taking place inside the house, Levi paced behind his Bronco, fretting over Popeye's long silence. A big part of his plan was to keep the killer's mind off his hostage by dickering with him until reinforcements arrived.

Although Levi prided himself on knowing Paul Eilert's history, and although he was confident of his own abilities, he was also professional enough to admit that there were agents better trained to free hostages. Right now, he'd like nothing better than to see a few of those agents. Eilert's silence didn't bode well for the girl.

What worried him the most was Eilert's total lack of remorse for his past crimes. Massaging his neck, Levi paced and wondered what was keeping Franzi and Billy Lee. As if conjured up by his thoughts, the young deputy reappeared.

Feeling some of his tension drain away, Levi hurried to meet him. "You've been gone long enough, Lee. Did you have problems getting through?"

Billy shook his head.

"So? How long before we get help?"

"Soon as they can. Your boss said to tell you he's had two marshals cooling their heels in Mojave all week. Said they'd be here as soon as they can make it."

"Mojave?" Levi flashed a rare smile. "That's right in the middle of the desert. Tully and Jim won't be too happy. Those guys are into bright lights and nightlife."

Billy didn't smile. He scanned the sky, waiting for Rick Poston's helicopter. Engrossed, he almost missed Levi's next question.

"Where did you leave Franzi? Is she back at Henry's cabin sulking?"

"Huh?" Billy jerked and passed a trembling hand over his skewed tie.

"What is it, Deputy?" Levi queried sharply. Then he recalled his own tugs of war with Franzi and shrugged. "Don't look so miserable, Lee. I promise not to ask what names she called me. Believe me, I've had a taste of her sassy mouth." Levi grimaced. That was a poor choice of words.

Billy stuffed his hands nervously into his pants pockets, then in another nervous gesture, yanked them out. Franzi's badge followed and landed with a plop at Levi's feet.

"What's this? Did you break the pin on your badge?"

Levi and Billy reached for the star at the same time. Levi was a fraction of a second faster. He started to hand it back, but his fingers encountered a crease. He looked came up sharply. "Isn't this Franzi's badge?"

Billy sighed and hung his head. Before he could speak, Eilert's voice boomed across the clearing.

"Hey, Hunter. I've got somethin' here that might interest you. A scrawny broad. Hair like a new penny, big green eyes and a mouth that won't quit."

Eilert's diabolical laugh drove the breath from Levi's lungs. "No, not Franzi," he whispered. Anguished eyes lighted on Billy, demanding a response.

Billy shook his head and backed away. Confirmation came from Franzi herself, though her voice sounded reedy and somewhat thin.

"Hunter! Hunter!" She cupped her hands to make the second one stronger. "Don't listen to him, Levi. He promised he'd let Lisa go in exchange for me. He's a liar. He's—"

"Shut up," Eilert shouted, blotting out whatever else she said.

The two men behind the Bronco heard a loud thwack, followed by a woman's cry of pain. Their eyes met and they both flinched.

Billy Lee's face fell. "Lordy. He's got both of them."

Levi grabbed the front of Billy's shirt and practically lifted him off the ground. "You knew what she planned to do. Didn't you? Didn't you?"

"Yes, sir." Billy admitted. "But if you knew her, you'd know there's no arguing when Franzi gets her mind made up." He struggled, trying to dislodge the marshal's bulldog grip. "Truth is, Marshal, I wanted her to succeed. She's a lot stronger than Lisa."

"If you think that, you don't know her very well, either." Levi released the younger man, catching him when he stumbled. In the past few moments, everything had changed. Levi thought he'd experienced fear before, but the terror gripping his heart now was the worst he'd ever felt. Everything had changed, and yet nothing could. The professional in him knew he dared not give Eilert what he wanted. The man in him wanted to hand over Fort Knox, if that was what it took.

So why, he was to ask himself later, did he break every one of his own rules when he picked up the bullhorn? "You harm one hair on her head, Eilert and there won't be enough left of you to hang."

Levi looked to Billy, wondering if his threat sounded as feeble to the deputy as it did to him.

"Aha!" Eilert crowed. "So she is your woman." He laughed savagely and seemed to relish describing graphically what he'd do to Franzi if Levi didn't get him a helicopter. He cut the time to eight hours.

Levi closed his eyes and ran a shaking hand over his stubbled cheeks. What would Adam think if he let Eilert escape to Mexico? But Levi now knew he'd do everything in his power to meet the felon's demand, even if he lost Adam's friendship, and his job, in the process.

In a voice so cold and deadly it belied his fear, Levi promised a deal. "I'll get a chopper. They'll take you anywhere in Mexico you say, no questions asked. But I'll see both the women safe first, or you won't set one foot on board. Got it?"

"You can't trust him, Levi," Franzi shouted. She gingerly ran a hand over her tender jaw. This time, Eilert would probably break it.

Her captor roared. Lisa threw herself into Franzi's arms and wailed, "Don't give him a reason to hit you again, Franzi! He'll kill you and I couldn't bear it."

Franzi patted Lisa and steeled herself for a blow that didn't come. She murmured soothingly and remembered to tell the girl what Billy had said about loving her. It bolstered her own spirits and kept her from thinking that Levi had been right the first time. Once Eilert got the chopper, he'd kill them, anyway.

"What's going on in there?" Levi called, praying Popeye hadn't punished Franzi for her impulsiveness. "Franzi, Lisa, everything okay?" His heart slammed erratically against his chest.

"We're fine," Franzi called back. Then she added, "I'm sorry—"

Eilert screamed at her to shut up.

Levi didn't realize he'd been holding his breath, waiting to hear proof she was alive. Now he let it out in a rush. He turned to Billy. "Get that helicopter, Lee."

"Already did," Billy mumbled.

"What?"

"Sheriff's orders. Was Eilert right, Hunter?" the young deputy probed. "Do you have feelings for Franzi?"

Levi started to deny it, then he stopped and clenched his hands. "I..." He coughed. "Uh... now that you mention it, I guess I do."

"Too bad." Billy sounded sympathetic.

"Now, look. Beneath that badge is quite a woman."

"Oh, I'm not saying anything against her, Marshal. I only meant it was too bad because of who you are. She hated what the men in her family did for a living. It's funny she agreed to help you, but I can't think it'll change anything."

"If a woman loves a man, his job shouldn't matter."

"It does to Franzi."

"Maybe she needs to see that all lawmen don't die." Levi rubbed his chin.

"I sure hope you get the chance to prove that. Myself, I'm gonna switch fields. When we get Lisa out of this mess—if she agrees to marry me, I mean—I want to better the odds for coming home to her and the baby every night."

Levi looked thoughtful. Would that kind of guarantee satisfy Franzi? He'd told her a man could drive to town for groceries and end up dead—like his father. "Enough of this talk, Billy,'' Levi said abruptly. ''We're both still bound by oath. We've got a job to do.''

Billy sighed. ''I think that's the attitude Franzi hates.''

Talking wouldn't change Levi's mind. Catching criminals and saving lives was his job. This time especially, he couldn't afford to fail.

Time dragged. Everyone was edgy when at last the throb of Poston's helicopter could be heard.

Eilert heard it, too. He let out a whoop. ''Hurry it up, Hunter. I got a hankering to eat breakfast in Mexico.''

Billy touched Levi's arm and pointed to a dark car moving slowly toward them, headlights extinguished. ''Looks like your friends.'' His face showed relief.

Levi didn't wait for the car to stop. He ran toward it and jerked open the door. The new arrivals were two of the best agents in the business, yet as Levi explained the situation, his voice shook. He couldn't forget the sound of Franzi's cry of pain when Eilert struck her.

Once the preliminaries were over, Levi grabbed his friends' radio and curtly instructed the pilot to circle overhead. Then he ordered Billy to round up Henry and the other deputy. The two agents shared a worried glance.

''What's with the chopper?'' Jim, the shorter of the two asked.

''Since we called you, Eilert's acquired another hostage. Two women. One's young and pregnant.''

Tully, a lanky man with ice-blue eyes, offered to get his rifle and a precision scope.

''We'll shoot as a last resort.'' Levi remained adamant. ''I'm banking Eilert will use one of those women for cover all the way to the chopper. I don't want any stray fire.''

The stockier agent, Jim, disagreed. ''If he's dragging a reluctant hostage and trying to deal with a weapon, he's bound to leave Tully an opening.''

Levi gazed at them for a long time, the muscles in his jaw working. "One of the women means a lot to me."

Tully swore. "Dammit, Hunter. That complicates everything."

"You think I don't know that?" Levi rubbed his jaw.

Jim stepped between them. "Okay, we'll play it your way for now, Levi. We'll keep our weapons out of sight."

As Billy and the others came back, Eilert screeched, "Hey, copper, what's takin' so long? You tryin' to run my chopper outta gas?"

"Not at all," Levi declared calmly. At the same time, he dispersed Henry and the younger deputy with a silent wave. "I'm deciding where we'll make the hostage transfer."

"Don't you worry none, Hunter. I'll decide that. You just don't be plannin' any surprises. Remember, I got nothin' to lose."

As if he could forget. Levi frowned in the direction of the taunting voice. Suddenly a woman screamed and something crashed inside the house.

"Lisa?" Billy ran back to Levi's side and called her name.

Eilert's laugh sent chills up everyone's spine. "Hunter, I just relieved your woman of a knife. She's damn lucky all I did was rough her up a bit."

Levi turned to the others. "He's lying. Eilert would love to force us into a reckless move." Cold sweat beaded his upper lip.

Billy turned white. "The knife was mine. Franzi hid it in her boot."

"Listen up, copper," Eilert screamed. "Green eyes just won herself the privilege of going to Mexico with me. I'm gonna hold this cutter tight against her pretty little throat. Anything, anything at all goes wrong, she's history." He ended his tirade with a high-pitched cackle.

"Stop him, Levi," they heard Franzi shout. "Any way you can." Then they heard her yelp of pain.

"Franzi, for crying out loud." Levi lifted his eyes to the gray sky beyond the hovering helicopter. "Please let me do everything right," he whispered, "because, so help me, I love her." It was a simple plea, and Levi felt calmer for having uttered it.

"Get that chopper down!" Eilert shouted. "Time for talk is over."

Levi motioned for the men to take their places. Tully and Jim were already crawling away on their bellies. He wanted them near the helicopter. Billy crouched behind the Bronco. His mission was to receive Lisa. Henry was halfway to the cabin; his instructions were to call fast for help if anything went awry.

Levi planned to hand Franzi to the second deputy, thus leaving him free to deal with Eilert. The plan was as good as he could make it.

But Jim and Tully weren't in place yet when the door flew open and Eilert pushed the two women onto the porch. He kept a tight grip on Lisa's collar with his right hand, while his left arm, knife in hand, encircled Franzi's neck. Lisa took small steps, sticking close to Eilert as she'd obviously been told to do. Franzi tried to wriggle free and lashed out at Eilert's leg with the heel of one boot.

The killer raised the knife a fraction. In the yellowish light falling from the porch lamp, Levi saw a thin line of blood trickle down her throat.

Popeye's move had the desired effect. Franzi stilled.

Fury blinded Levi until he reminded himself that any foolish action on his part would bring swift retribution to Franzi. But whatever happened, Eilert would pay, he swore. And pay. And pay.

Levi spread his empty hands and moved into sight, to the left of the Bronco. Less than six yards separated him from Eilert. As he focused on the killer, sweat soaked his shirt and his palms grew damp. Next to Franzi's slender frame, Eilert looked like a tank.

Suddenly, without warning, in a move calculated to throw his enemies off balance, Eilert spun Lisa away from himself and threw her into Levi's chest.

Wavering for only an instant, Levi steadied her, took one step back and transferred her to Billy as planned. Eilert used those few seconds to draw a pistol from his belt with his now free right hand.

Even though they'd discussed the probability, Levi wasn't prepared to see the steely barrel jammed into Franzi's ribs. Careful to match his quarry step for step, Levi closed his ears to Eilert's taunts. As discreetly as possible, he motioned for Tully to stay out of sight with his rifle.

Franzi had to walk on tiptoe to keep from feeling the knife, but somehow the strain on Levi's face affected her more than her own plight. One misstep and they'd both be dead. She couldn't let that happen.

After walking for what seemed an interminable amount of time, Franzi saw that she and Eilert had reached the first step of a portable stair that led to the opening of the helicopter. The stairs had been one of his demands. She stumbled twice. Both times the knife pricked her skin. She was beyond caring. Her thoughts were on saving Hunter. She must not fail this time.

Suddenly they were at the entryway. Ducking to avoid the whip of the rotors, the man holding Franzi turned briefly to make sure no one was inside but the pilot.

For a second, Levi thought Popeye was going to release Franzi. But then he saw the knife move and he reacted to Franzi's cry of pain by charging up the ramp like a crazed bull.

"Stop or I swear I'll kill her now!" Eilert roared.

It was enough to check Levi's forward motion and stop him from reaching for his thirty-eight. Eilert dragged Franzi inside. He was trying to close the door when Levi launched himself at the opening, his only thought to free Franzi, whatever it took.

Eilert shot him twice at close range, but not before the knife had changed hands. Levi staggered back, blood seeping through his shirt, his hands slick with it.

Franzi screamed and kicked out at Eilert. She couldn't let Levi die. She loved him and his fate was in her hands.

Popeye's massive arm tightened, choking off her wind. Slowly Franzi's world went black.

CHAPTER TEN

AS FRANZI REGAINED consciousness, she saw two strang
men above her grappling with Eilert. One was wresting th
gun from his hand, while the other roughly pulled the felo
into a half nelson from behind. She sucked air into her tor
tured lungs and realized that the strangers were there to help
Where was Levi?

Vaguely she remembered watching him slide down th
steps. And she remembered seeing the blood.

It took a herculean effort to crawl out from under th
men's feet. The wail of sirens had shocked her into action
As an aid car and ambulance rolled up and squealed to
stop beyond the helicopter, her heart beat a quick tattoo.

Doing more stumbling than walking, Franzi made he
way down the ramp to the ground. The double click o
handcuffs being snapped around Eilert's wrists brought
giddy kind of relief. She hardly heard Eilert cursing an
swearing vengeance as the two agents manhandled him pas
her. She just wanted to find Levi.

Billy Lee appeared and helped shackle the belligeren
Popeye to the base of the helicopter. Franzi gave one las
shudder, and from then on, Eilert ceased to matter.

Off to her right, a team of white-coated medics wer
loading Levi onto a gurney. His eyes were closed. Franz
could see his thick lashes lying still against his pasty cheeks
He looked like death. She had to fight for breath again. Bu
then, as the medics ripped away his bloody shirt, she saw hi

chest move. When they exposed the ragged wound on his shoulder, Franzi felt the bile rise in her throat.

Something inside her screamed that it was unfair for a man who disliked guns as much as he did to suffer two gaping gunshot wounds. What she didn't realize was that her own shirt almost rivaled his for blood.

When one of the medics saw her he tried to render aid, but she shook him off. "Leave me," she commanded, twisting to keep Levi in sight. "Why aren't you doing something for him?"

"Ma'am," the young medic said, "there's already two fellows doing that. Your injury looks serious, too."

She put a hand to her neck and remembered Eilert's nicking her. If she had listened to Levi, none of this would have happened. She felt awash in shame. "It's just a scratch," she mumbled. "Nothing to worry about."

Levi's eyes half opened then. Though groggy, he gazed up at her. His mouth curved in what might have passed for a weak smile had he not been clenching his teeth against the pain. "Something you guys should know about this lady," he whispered hoarsely. "When she calls something a scratch, it's like calling the Mississippi a creek."

His audience didn't react to his attempt at humor because the effort to talk brought on a new spurt of blood. One of his attendants curtly ordered Franzi to leave.

Levi looked at the medic applying a pressure pack to his shoulder. "Make sure you check her over," he managed.

The other medic, taking Levi's blood pressure, frowned. "Would you mind letting us take a look? His concern for you is causing him stress."

Franzi submitted at last and Levi visibly relaxed. She only took her eyes off him when Lisa came flying around the corner of the Bronco.

Disheveled and wild-looking, the younger woman clasped Franzi's hand to her heart. "Oh, Franzi! When Eilert said he was going to take you to Mexico with him and that door started to close, I thought I'd die."

"Ouch." Franzi squirmed away from the determined medic cleaning her cuts. Whatever he used stung worse than when Levi had dumped whiskey on her arm. The sting brought a vivid memory of their kiss. "I'm fine," she insisted. "I may have a bruise or two where Eilert tried to choke me," she said absently to Lisa, "but that's minor compared...compared to..." Her gaze locked on Levi's still form.

She was distracted by Billy Lee, who loped toward them. Happily he slid his arms around the dark-haired girl's thickening waist and openly nuzzled her neck. "Lordy, what an ordeal. It's a miracle no one died." He smiled and kissed Lisa outright.

She blushed and slapped his hand away, but he only laughed and grinned at Franzi. "I told her everything," he said softly. "She forgives me—and we're getting married! Do we have your blessing?"

Franzi gave a slight nod, to the medic's dismay. "Of course! I'm so happy for both of you." Her voice faltered, and tears brimmed in her eyes. She had some confessions of her own, but the man to whom she needed to confess was in no condition to listen.

Levi did hear bits and pieces of the conversation going on around him, as he drifted in and out of consciousness. The reference to marriage stuck in his brain. Images of Franzi, draped in ivory satin with her coppery hair peeking provocatively out from under a lacy veil, floated just beyond his reach.

He imagined his family accepting her into their close-knit circle, and tried to smile. Then the pain bore him back into darkness. He surfaced, feeling anxious that his boisterous brothers-in-law not tease her unmercifully about raising mules. Good men, they meant well. He must impress on them how vulnerable she was underneath.

Loud unfamiliar voices drove away the images Levi fought to maintain. Someone, perhaps the man ramming a hot poker into his shoulder, was talking surgery, not marriage. Who needed surgery? Please, not Franzi! Levi's heart hammered, and he battled the cold invading his limbs.

A second needle bit deep into his arm. He blinked up into a sea of faces. Jim and Tully, his old friends, stood looking gravely down on him.

"Appears one of those slugs is lodged against your shoulder blade, buddy," Jim murmured. "Hang in. These guys reserved you a first-class suite at the new hospital in town."

Tully winked at Franzi and missed the frightened look in her eyes. "Some guys get all the luck. Jim and I had to make do with Mojave."

Jim jabbed his taller friend in the ribs. He put a quieter question to Levi. "If it's okay with you, we thought we'd hustle Eilert's extradition to Salt Lake. The sooner we book this creep, the sooner we can start proceedings."

Levi nodded. "Promise you won't lose him." His lips were white, tinged with blue around the edges.

Franzi glanced over in surprise. "You two are U.S. Marshals?"

"Yes, ma'am," they responded in unison.

"Well, I hope you build an airtight case." She shivered. "I'd hate to think he'd ever be on the loose again. You can count on my testimony, as one of his hostages."

"No." Levi's command was forceful enough to gain everyone's attention.

"Now, Levi," cautioned Tully, "don't be too hasty. I know you think you've got charges enough to keep him on ice, but when it comes to a lowlife like Eilert, you can't have too much firsthand testimony."

"Yeah, Hunter," agreed Jim, who had begun a lazy appraisal of Franzi. "And it never hurts to have an attractive witness. You know it's great for jury sympathy."

Although Levi was clearly not in any condition to resist, resist he did. He struggled up onto his good elbow, drawing a worried exclamation from the medic, who grabbed for the IV. In a voice stronger than any they'd heard yet, he snarled, "We've got an open-and-shut case against Paul Eilert. You don't need her to testify. Period." His hot gaze skipped over Franzi and centered on the men.

A look passed between them. "Okay. Whatever you say, buddy." The two men shot apologetic glances Franzi's way.

All of a sudden, she was furious. Even practically on his deathbed, Levi Hunter was arrogant. Full of that stupid chivalry, when chivalry was neither solicited nor wanted. She forgot totally that only moments ago she'd been sick with worry. "What's the matter, Hunter? Are you afraid if I testify you won't get credit for the collar?"

Levi watched her pale face slip from view as he collapsed back on the bed. What was happening? He'd been envisioning them living happily ever after. Why didn't she just stop talking and kiss him? He'd thought of nothing but holding her safely in his arms from the moment Eilert had shoved her out onto the porch. He'd tell her, too, if her face would just quit fading in and out.

"You needn't glare at me," she sniffed, misreading his pain for disapproval. "You'll be up in no time. They won't run out of bad guys while you recover." Her voice shook. "—I'm sure you'll collect that one-liner yet. But not in Alano County."

Levi frowned. Her speech was way too long. He still hadn't gotten that kiss, and her lovely face was beginning to spin.

Not only that, but it was growing cold again. So cold he didn't think he'd ever get warm. Before he lost her altogether, he tugged at the medic's coat and mumbled, "She's stubborn as a mule. Always gets the last word. You'd think she might at least thank me for saving her life."

Franzi's heart stilled as he fell into unconsciousness. Thank him? Thank him for scaring her witless? For stopping a bullet? For almost dying?

Her hand flew to the thick bandage on her neck. He'd saved her life all right, and at great risk to his own. But didn't the fool know her fears had never been for herself? Always for him?

As they began to load him into the ambulance, she turned blindly and clutched Billy Lee for support. Twice Levi had saved her life, when all she ever wanted was to keep *him* alive. And now he might die.

Franzi dropped Billy's arm and rushed to Levi's side. She'd breathe life into him now if she could. Lord help her, but she loved him. Tears trickled down her cheeks and splashed onto his limp hand. She'd really tried not to care for him. And now she couldn't bear to lose him.

A medic set her roughly aside. "He's losing a lot of blood, ma'am. If anyone wants anything more from him, it'll have to wait."

She raised pleading eyes to the little group of bystanders. "I didn't mean... I don't always have the last word." Tears streaked her cheeks.

"It's the drug talking," Tully said gently, handing her a clean handkerchief. "Why don't you come into town with us and we'll take your deposition? Then you can go to the hospital to visit him."

"Yes." Her worried gaze flew to the rapidly disappearing ambulance. She clutched Lisa's arm. "You'll be needed, too. Where's Henry? He'll keep an eye on things until we return."

"I'm right over here, Missy D." The old man stepped from behind his pickup clutching Pirate's collar. The dog growled and lunged at Eilert. Henry kept him just out of reach. "Once they take the bad dude away, Pirate and me will get on with chores." His wrinkled face split into a grin. "I delivered two right pretty spotted mules while you was gallivantin' in the hills."

Franzi wasn't even able to drum up enthusiasm for the news. "They'll be able to save him, won't they?" She whirled and grabbed Billy's sleeve.

"Don't ask me." The young deputy unpinned his badge and shoved it into her hand. "I'm resigning, Sheriff. But I'll drive you and Lisa to town."

Franzi's hand flew to her empty vest. "I forgot. You have my badge. I'll leave them both with Daryl. I was crazy to think I could save anyone." Her lips trembled.

Billy looked uncomfortable. "Hunter has your badge. It fell out of my pocket. But aren't you being too hard on yourself, Franzi? Everything turned out fine."

"How can you say that?" She climbed into his truck and leaned her head back against the seat. "Levi has every right to hate me for interfering. Let's go, Billy. I have to see him. I have to apologize for... for a lot of things."

Billy stepped on the gas and pulled in behind the dark sedan driven by Jim. Eilert was being forcibly restrained in the back seat by Tully. "Let's follow these guys to the jail. You ladies can give your statements so they can get that madman on a plane to Salt Lake. I, for one, won't rest easy until he's behind bars."

Franzi shook her head. "Drop me at the hospital."

"Hunter'll probably already be in surgery."

She bit her lip. "Maybe so, Billy, but if there's a chance I can see him first..." Her voice trailed off.

Billy started to say more, but Lisa placed a hand on his arm and shook her head. Closing his mouth, Billy turned into the street leading to the new hospital.

"Thanks." At the entrance, Franzi leapt out. There was no sign of the ambulance. "I'll be along later," she promised.

Not caring what she looked like with her bloody shirt and flyaway hair, Franzi burst through the hospital's double doors and grabbed the first person in a uniform she happened to see.

"U.S. Marshal Levi Hunter," she begged the startled nurse. "Can you direct me? I need to see him right away."

A slim eyebrow shot up, as the woman took in her disheveled appearance. "Are you family?"

"No." Franzi realized she had nothing official with her except Billy's badge. She waved it. "We're colleagues," she lied.

The woman's eyes darkened. "Then I suppose it's all right for me to tell you—he's gone. No, no," she reassured at Franzi's gasp. "Not dead. Just gone. Dr. Billings talked to your boss, and it was decided to fly Mr. Hunter back to Salt Lake City immediately."

"My boss?" Franzi froze. She was trying to make sense of what the nurse was saying.

"You did say you and Marshal Hunter were colleagues, didn't you?" The pretty nurse was beginning to look nervous, as though she'd given classified information to a nut and could see herself losing her job over it.

Franzi dredged up a smile. "My name is DeLisle. I'm the local acting sheriff. Why would they take Marshal Hunter so far away?"

"Oh, Ms. DeLisle. I recognize your name." The woman shook her head. "I don't know the particulars. Something about a messy trial, the bullet going in at a bad angle and a long recovery. Dr. Billings has left the hospital, but you're welcome to come back and talk with him."

"That's okay." Franzi shrugged awkwardly. "Do you know the name of the hospital where Hunter was being transferred? I'd like to send flowers."

"No. Sorry." The nurse edged away. "You look quite pale yourself, Ms. DeLisle. You have blood seeping through that bandage. I suggest you stop by our emergency room and have it checked."

Franzi declined. "This case still has a lot of loose ends. I have people waiting at the jail."

"Well, good luck. Your Mr. Hunter seemed upset when he first arrived. He kept calling out, like he was trying to warn someone."

"Amanda?" Franzi asked, unable to help herself. "Did he want Amanda?"

The woman in white frowned. "No, that wasn't the name. Did anyone die in this shoot-out?" she asked suddenly.

Franzi's heart did a cartwheel. Her mouth opened, but she couldn't speak. Couldn't ask if it was *her* name he'd called.

"That's all right. You don't need to tell me if it's painful."

Franzi's lips trembled. "No one died, thanks to Hunter." It was the truth, and she suddenly saw how many of his own rules he'd broken in the process. He'd broken them for her.

"I'm relieved to hear you didn't lose anyone." The nurse brightened. "Like me, you seem to have chosen a job where death's always hovering in the wings." Her touch was warm against Franzi's cold hand. "But we can't beat ourselves up about it, can we? Not if we've done our best. Say, I only just realized why your name is so familiar. That other time—it was your dad, wasn't it? And I know your brother recently died. You probably think I have some nerve, lecturing *you* on survival. Take care, okay? I've got to go."

After the nurse left, Franzi stood for several moments, mulling over what had been said. Beating herself up? Wasn't that exactly what she'd been doing every day since her father's death? That day she had followed orders like a deputy should. But maybe nothing would have changed if she'd stayed behind.

An elderly woman accidentally bumped into her, then stopped and asked if everything was all right. Franzi managed to pull herself together enough to reassure the stranger. She left for the jail with a lighter step. Yes, she was a survivor.

Suddenly Franzi couldn't wait to tell Levi about her discovery. She *wanted* to be called to Salt Lake City to give testimony; she'd talk to the other marshals and insist. She'd finally begun to put her personal demons to rest and she knew she could handle the trial. Then maybe she and Levi could start to think about a future. But when she reached the jail, she found the two marshals and the prisoner gone. Only Billy and Lisa were there, waiting impatiently.

"Jim left an address for you to mail a written statement, Franzi," Billy said without preamble. "You were gone so long and they had a chance to get Eilert on a charter. I even had time to settle things with Daryl. I said you'd give him my badge. In case you're interested, he took it well. He offered me a job on his ranch."

Lisa stepped forward. "I know it's presumptuous, Franzi, but can I stay with you until Billy and I get married?"

"Of course. Why would you even ask? I'll miss you, Lisa. It has nothing to do with Gage." Franzi's tone was wistful. "I'm sorry I doubted you."

Lisa threw her arms around Franzi and hugged her. "This whole thing has been a nightmare. I'm so glad Billy found a different job. And Commissioner Parker said to tell you thanks. He's trying to find a new sheriff."

"I guess I can't leave Daryl in the lurch, but he needs to know I may be called to testify soon. By the way, they've flown Hunter back to Salt Lake, too." She paused, then said in a wondering tone, "Maybe this whole thing was a figment of our imaginations."

"It was real all right." Lisa shivered. "You've got the wounds to prove it. I thought I'd die when you spoke up and Eilert hit you. I wouldn't be half so brave."

"Speaking of brave..." Billy looked serious. "Can you believe Hunter throwing himself at that door, knowing he faced a loaded gun? I sure hope he's all right. Hey—" he snapped his fingers "—I have a telephone number for his boss if you want it, Franzi. Remember the call he had me make from Henry's? Here's the number he gave me. The guy was nice. He might thank Hunter for you." Billy hustled both women toward the door.

Franzi accepted the paper wordlessly. She worried all the way home about whether or not she should call. By late afternoon, her nerves were shot. She relented and dialed the number with shaking fingers.

Levi's boss, Cal Jones, did seem nice. Not only did he give her the information on Levi's condition, he promised to call her when Levi came out of surgery. In the course of conversation Franzi found an opening to inquire about Amanda Farrell. Although not yet out of the woods, she had been taken off the critical list. Franzi sighed. The news would be heartening for Levi.

In the endless wait for an account of his progress, Franzi vacuumed up the glass from the gun cabinet and prevailed on Henry to dispose of a good number of Gage's guns. It was the least she could do for Hunter, she thought in the midst of her cleaning frenzy, and she added it to the growing list of things to tell him.

It was nearly midnight when Cal called to say Levi seemed weak but was holding his own.

Franzi was too tired by then to do anything except fall directly into bed. Once she was there, though, she couldn't sleep. Awake or dozing, memories of the gray-eyed marshal plagued her. The few tender moments they'd shared continued to haunt her. She was now able to accept that she probably couldn't have changed the course of events that had led to her father's death. Yet she knew with equal certainty that things might have gone differently for Levi if she *hadn't* interfered with his mission. It didn't help, during this long restless night, that she imagined his scent still clung to her sheets.

At dawn, she gave up her efforts to sleep. She stripped her bed right down to the mattress and threw it all into the wash. When the sun streaked the sky over Mount Markham with layers of pink and gold, she stood under a steaming shower, but she couldn't wash away her memories of the man from Utah.

Nothing worked. Even though it was still too early, she called Cal again, just to assure herself that Levi had made it through the night.

He had. She put great store in the fact that Cal said he was grumpy as a bear. Enough to race right into town to send him flowers and a note of apology. It took her an hour to decide on salmon-colored roses. Red reminded her too much of blood. White was embarrassingly virginal. Carnations were too feminine. Daisies lacked the intensity her apology needed. The clerk filling out the order obviously found her behavior odd, but Franzi didn't care.

Wording the apology was much harder. She agonized over it while three other customers were served, and in the end, asked the woman to simply sign her name. Brimming over with uncertainty, she fled the shop. She'd managed to convince herself that the florist card didn't have room for everything that needed to be said.

Besides, why make the nurses at his hospital twitter? Soon, at the trial, they would meet face-to-face. Hadn't Cal said the prosecutor intended to push Eilert's case to the top of the docket? She and Lisa could be called to testify in a matter of weeks. And if it took longer? Well, she could apologize when he called her about the flowers. At least, she assumed he'd call; if someone sent her roses, she would.

At first the days dragged and she made excuses for his not phoning. Then as they flew by and melted into weeks, Franzi admitted that perhaps he wasn't going to forgive her. Spring gave way to summer, and she knew he never would.

Because Lisa was often off with Billy and rarely home, Franzi installed an answering machine to take her calls. Not that she expected one from Levi now, but someone would notify her when she was needed at the trial. She had sloughed her outside duties off on Henry long enough.

Franzi refused to guide pack trains for another two weeks. Instead, from sunup to sundown, she worked breaking young mules to saddle, while at night she did the paperwork for her temporary job as sheriff. She'd agreed to stay on until Daryl could find a replacement. Fortunately nothing of much significance happened in the county during the time, and the tedious tasks matched her mood perfectly. It suited her to fall into bed every night, too exhausted for unwanted dreams.

Franzi had lost track of how long it had been since Eilert's capture. She was shocked when Billy and Lisa approached her in the corral one hot afternoon and asked if she'd stand up at their wedding the following Saturday.

"So soon?" She blinked away her surprise.

"Billy's folks are giving us two weeks in San Francisco for a honeymoon, Franzi. Isn't that wonderful?" The bloom of happiness on Lisa's cheeks contrasted with Franzi's sudden pallor. "I've hardly ever been out of Jessup," Lisa continued, "and I've never spent the night in a hotel." She blushed, and her cheeks grew even rosier. "Uh... Billy thought it would be nice for us to go before the baby comes."

Franzi turned to Billy, who stood by grinning from ear to ear. "Billy, what if any of us are needed to testify in Salt Lake City while you're in San Francisco? I don't want to be a spoilsport, but shouldn't you hold off on your plans?"

Billy raked a hand through his hair. "Uh, um... they won't need us." He ran one finger beneath his shirt collar.

"That's ridiculous," Franzi said. "Of course they will. Where did you come by such a notion?"

"Hunter." Even as he said it, Billy looked as if he wished he hadn't.

"Hunter?" Franzi echoed the name. "Oh? And I suppose he calls you all the time?"

"Uh, no," Billy hedged. "Once or twice. This time, I called him—to invite him to the wedding." He reached out an arm and pulled Lisa into a loose embrace.

Franzi steadied herself against the fence. Simply hearing his name sent shivers of longing through her body. A longing to hear his voice. A greater longing to see him—and touch him.

Pirate trotted across the paddock and jumped at her, almost sending her onto her backside. Franzi regained her calm. As she'd always done, she resorted to cynicism to hide her pain. "So, I imagine our big-city cop decided his country counterparts have nothing of value to offer at his precious trial."

Billy shook his head sadly. "You still don't get it, do you, Franzi? Hunter arranged it so you wouldn't have to go. He told the prosecutor you'd been through too much already. You should be grateful." He started to turn Lisa away, then stopped and looked back. "The mystery to me is why he went to all the trouble of protecting you, the way you act. 'Course, I said to him that day, you'd never accept his profession."

Franzi gave a chilly laugh. "I sincerely doubt he cared, Billy. Born lawmen are immune to feelings. All they care about is their mission—then the next one and the next. I was a fool for thinking he was different." Her eyes darkened. Became remote.

"Some maybe, but not Hunter," Billy insisted stubbornly. "I saw his face when Eilert had you. From then on, he was like a crazy man. Heaven help any of us if we'd screwed up."

"Certainly," Franzi sniffed. "It all came down to duty. Goodness knows, a lawman never shirks his duty."

"Maybe the folks in Jessup are right about you, Franzi. Maybe you spend too much time with these mules. Maybe you can't feel human emotions anymore. If you can tear yourself away and want to act sociable for a change, the offer's still open for Saturday."

"Billy, wait," Franzi called as the lovers walked away. "I wouldn't miss it." She fidgeted with the gate closure. "Uh . . ."she stammered, "di-did Levi say if he was coming for sure?"

Billy shrugged. "I hope you're not asking so you can avoid him. I never took you for a coward, Franzi."

She flushed and looked away. She *was* afraid to see him again. But the people in Jessup were wrong. She didn't hide out with her mules because she didn't care. She did it because she cared too much.

For the remainder of the week, she wrestled with Billy's accusation. All the things she couldn't forget about Levi Hunter nagged at her. His innate goodness. His gentleness with animals. His tenderness with her and with the young mountain climbers. His teasing.

Billy had it backward. It wasn't that she didn't want to see him again. In fact, she wanted to see him whether or not he was a lawman. She had loved her dad, her uncle and Gage—and now, Levi.

The day of the wedding arrived before Franzi was prepared. Oh, she'd bought the right dress, the slip and new shoes—all the trappings to bolster her ego. Levi was very much on her mind as she washed her hair, then brushed it dry. On impulse, she decided to leave it loose, as he'd once suggested. Pride dictated that this one time he would see her looking like a woman. If he showed up.

She stepped into her high-heeled pumps and stared in the mirror at the unfamiliar apparition in the glamorous green dress. Franzi knew then that if he didn't come, she'd go to him and at least clear her conscience.

FRANZI HAD JUST STEPPED from her truck in front of the chapel when she ran into Kendra Peters. Her friend broke into a wide reassuring smile. "Wow! Don't you look like a million bucks, Franzi DeLisle!" Kendra drew back, giving her friend a thorough once-over. "I suppose that drop-dead handsome man you chased out of my house a couple of months ago is the reason for this big change." She winked at her husband.

"Certainly not," Franzi denied, her face aflame. "We haven't even spoken since he completed his mission."

Kendra turned to her husband. "But I thought you said Billy told you—"

Jared interrupted her with a hurried question about parking.

Kendra answered him and doggedly kept at it. "I thought from the way you sounded, wedding bells were—"

"Say, isn't that Daryl Parker?" Once again Jared interrupted.

The heavyset man doffed his hat as he approached. "I've been trying to call you, Franzi-girl. Yesterday I got us a new temporary sheriff. You can come by Monday and turn in your badge."

"Do I know him, Daryl?" Franzi feigned interest.

The commissioner shifted his bulk and waved to someone entering the church. "I'd better go if I want a decent seat."

"What do you suppose that was all about?" Franzi laughed as he hurried off. "Do I know the man he hired or not?"

Mischief lit Kendra's eyes. "What if Daryl hired your friend?"

"Don't kid yourself, Kendra. Levi would never leave the city to work here."

Before Kendra could respond, the groom hurried over to them. "Hey, guys—" he straightened his tie and fooled with the matching hankie peeking out of his breast pocket "—what do you think? Do I look all right? Gosh, I'm nervous."

Franzi gave serious study to her former deputy's immaculate suit and sky-blue tie. She knew the tie matched Lisa's dress, but it also gave color to Billy's pale eyes. "You look smashing, William. Too mature to be called Billy today. Calm down."

"Maybe Will-yum knows," Kendra drawled.

He gave a last yank on his cuffs. "Maybe I know what?"

"Did Daryl hire Franzi's marshal friend to be our new sheriff?"

"Kendra, I swear," Franzi burst out in exasperation. "You have a one-track mind. There's nothing he'd want here."

"What if he *was* to be our sheriff? Could you be civil?" Billy asked.

Franzi clapped a hand to her mouth. The idea stole her breath. She wanted to tell Billy she would gladly accept Levi on any terms, at any time. "I don't . . . Is he—?" she stammered.

"Well, why don't you ask him?" Billy broke in. "There he is." Then someone called from the chapel and he left.

Franzi whirled and stared. Indeed, Levi was just climbing out of one of Jessup's cabs. The day Cal had sent a stranger to pick up the Bronco was the day she'd really given up hope that Levi would ever come back.

And didn't he look marvelous today—especially compared to when she'd seen him last! The dark blue suit and white shirt set off a healthy tan. He looked fit and rested.

Jared rushed to help Levi with the large gift he was carrying. The two stood by the curb and talked like old friends.

Franzi couldn't stop staring. Not even when Jared took the gift toward the church and left Levi standing there alone. She wanted to memorize the shape of his lean face and the set of his broad shoulders—for those endless days when he'd be gone again.

Kendra went right on talking—as if Franzi's world hadn't just turned topsy-turvy. "I hope Jared remembered to tell him we heard from the boy he helped rescue," she was saying, "Matt's already back in college."

Levi was walking in their direction, and Franzi didn't hear one word Kendra said. Her mind scrambled to form the apology he was due. Until this moment, she hadn't known how hard it would be to deliver. When he said hello and complimented her on her dress, all she could do was gape.

Amused, Kendra reached past Franzi and pumped Levi's hand. "Nice to see you again, Marshal."

He tore his gaze from Franzi's face. "Not Marshal now." He released Kendra's fingers and shot Franzi a troubled look.

"Oh?" Kendra pounced, giving Franzi a triumphant smile. "Have you come to be Jessup's new sheriff?"

His eyes bored into Franzi's. "I've come for a wedding."

"Nothing more?" Kendra sounded disappointed.

His lips flirted with a smile. "Well, I owe this lady a pint of fine Irish whiskey." He pulled an amber bottle from his coat pocket.

Red-faced, Franzi nibbled her lip. "I think Jared's calling you, Kendra."

Kendra tossed her dark curls. "Just like that man to expect me to miss gossip in the making," she grumbled. "But you'd better tell me later, Franzi. Hey, they're calling you, too. After all, you're Lisa's attendant." When they didn't budge, she left without them.

"Mind if I tag along?" Levi asked Franzi. "I'm standing up for Billy."

"You are?" Franzi sounded surprised.

Levi spread his hands. "Did he tell you Eilert got ninety-nine years?"

"You aren't going to be Jessup's sheriff, are you?" she asked abruptly.

Levi felt his shirt pocket and drew out her old badge. "Would you hate it if I did?"

"Of course not." She ran a finger over the deep bullet crease. "If you'd ever called, I'd have told you I learned that having a short time with someone you love is better than having no time with him at all." She blushed furiously.

"Him? Are we talking DeLisle men here?" He touched her flaming cheek.

"No." She lowered her eyes. "I mean—"

"Don't," he cautioned. "Don't qualify it, please. I've agreed to be sheriff here temporarily. To replace the other...uh, temporary sheriff. Only because my other reason for coming back to Jessup seemed chancy."

"Oh," she said breathlessly. "What reason was that?"

"To take a look at grazing land," he said offhandedly.

"In mule country?" She tightened her fingers on the bottle until her knuckles turned white.

The teasing light—the one Franzi had discovered she missed so much—returned to his eyes. "I picked up a couple of sweet little Appaloosa mares from my brother-in-law.

You wouldn't know of anyone interested in perfecting a prettier mule, would you?"

"How much for the mares?" Her own eyes gleamed.

"Oh, they aren't for sale."

"What exactly did you mean then?" Confusion brought a frown. "Surely *you* aren't wanting the first foal? I have it on good authority you don't like anything about the homely beasts."

Levi winced. "While I was laid up, I found myself at loose ends." He reached for his inside pocket and produced a thin book, which he held up for her inspection. "I had time to read and digest this."

She glanced at the title. *The Unappreciated Beast of Burden—The Mule*. Franzi threw back her head and laughed. "You actually read that?"

Looking miffed, he stuffed it back into his pocket. "Cover to cover."

Her lips twitched. "You and your manuals. Now I suppose you're an expert?"

"No. But I figure my partner will fill in the rest."

"Partner?" Franzi's smile faded. "Tully? Or Jim?"

"Never. They haven't recovered from Mojave. No...I have a certain lady in mind. But she's kind of mulish herself. However, the book says even the most stubborn creature can learn—with loving patience." Levi let his words sink in as he deliberately separated a long strand of her coppery hair and looped it around his index finger. "I'm a patient man, Franzi," he whispered, tugging her face to within an inch of his own.

Her breath caught. "You're calling me stubborn again, aren't you, Hunter?"

He bent his head and his lips brushed hers. "Levi. Call me Levi."

Franzi sighed and followed his lips as he eased away. "Uh Levi...if I have so many faults, why would you want me fo a partner?"

"The roses." He helped himself to her lips again, nib bling at the corners. "No lady ever sent me flowers be fore."

"They were a token apology. But when you didn't call..."

"I couldn't until I had Eilert put away for good." He kissed her eyes closed. "I couldn't stand the thought of yo being anywhere near that monster. And I knew you'd com rushing in, demanding to testify, if you knew when the tria was on. Besides, I figured feelings like ours were stron enough to outlast a little delay." He kissed her again, he throat, her forehead, her cheeks.

"You're right, they have. But Levi—" She moaned. " can't think when you kiss me."

"Good." Levi's mouth covered hers. The kiss was lon and satisfying.

Thoroughly dazed, she blinked up at him when it ended.

"Didn't you know I'd be back to have the last word?" h teased. "I never have yet, you know?" Grinning, he re leased her curl unexpectedly.

Franzi landed back on the heels of her new pumps, an she wobbled, but Levi steadied her. Just then Billy Le stepped out beneath the portico and motioned wildly.

Franzi grasped Levi's lapels. She still said nothing.

Levi acknowledged Billy's wave, obviously surprised a her silence. "I do believe we're making progress with thi last-word thing." He bent to kiss her nose.

She suddenly wrinkled it and leaned back. "We'll dis cuss this partnership later. After we see Billy and Lisa mar ried. Anyway, I don't think it'll work."

"Is it the badge?" he asked, sounding worried.

She shook her head.

"Then what? I studied mules. I replaced your whiskey. *I love you.*"

"But you don't have any faults, Hunter!" she cried, "and I have *lots.*"

"Levi," he reminded her. "Call me Levi. And I'm definitely not perfect."

Franzi looked doubtful.

"Are you forgetting my lustful behavior?" he whispered. "All because of you and those damnable satin sheets. And if that's not enough, remember my tracking skills?" He edged her toward the church.

Her mouth opened and closed, but no sound came.

Levi gave her one of his crooked smiles. "Franzi, this is no time to give *me* the last word. I was hoping maybe we could set our own wedding date today."

Franzi's eyes widened. Her breath escaped in a whoosh.

He hid a smile. Well, maybe he *could* get used to having the last word after all, he thought, backing her tight against the door she was trying desperately to open. Deliberately he ran his tongue around the bright pink shell of her ear.

"Next Saturday might be nice. Since I've more or less already invited my family."

"But you can't." Franzi looked aghast. "We can't."

"You don't love me?" He frowned. "But everyone said—"

"I do love you," she rushed to say, "but maybe love isn't enough."

Levi rolled his eyes skyward. "I suspected my having the last word was too good to be true. Are you absolutely positive you love me, Franzi DeLisle?"

She nodded rapidly.

It occurred to Levi then that there were more pleasant ways of making sure one had the last word. Which he set about proving as he captured her protesting lips again.

The kiss well and truly left Franzi speechless.

Levi pulled reluctantly away and reminded her they had a wedding to attend.

Stubbornly she tugged his face back to hers.

He hesitated. In a way, she was still getting the last word—or was she? "Lady," he groaned, as she strained against him. "Ma'am...oh, Sheriff." He gave in. "Franzi," he pleaded. "Does this mean we have a lifetime to work together on perfection?"

This time Levi chose to take her fiery kiss as acquiescence. Especially when the recently retired DeLisle badge fell to the ground between them, and Franzi didn't even notice.

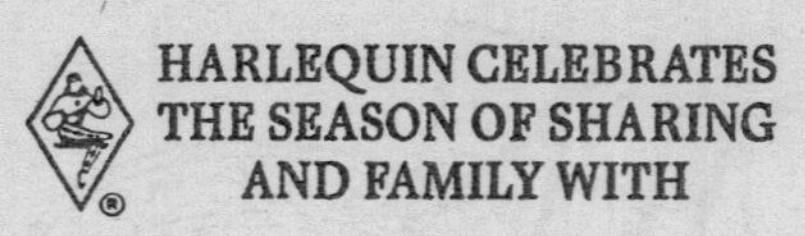

Harlequin introduces the latest member in its family of seasonal collections. Following in the footsteps of the popular *My Valentine, Just Married* and *Harlequin Historical Christmas Stories,* we are proud to present FRIENDS, FAMILIES, LOVERS. A collection of three new contemporary romance stories about America at its best, about welcoming others into the circle of love.... Stories to warm your heart...

By three leading romance authors:

KATHLEEN EAGLE
SANDRA KITT
RUTH JEAN DALE

Available in October, wherever
Harlequin books are sold.

THANKS